PENGUIN BOOKS

THE SECRET DIARY
OF LAURA PALMER

△ TWIN PEAKS △
A
BOOK

THE SECRET DIARY
OF LAURA PALMER

As seen by Jennifer Lynch

PENGUIN BOOKS

PENGUIN BOOKS

Published by the Penguin Group
Penguin Books Ltd, 27 Wrights Lane, London W8 5TZ, England
Viking Penguin, a division of Penguin Books USA Inc.
375 Hudson Street, New York, New York 10014, USA
Penguin Books Australia Ltd, Ringwood, Victoria, Australia
Penguin Books Canada Ltd, 2801 John Street, Markham, Ontario, Canada L3R 1B4
Penguin Books (NZ) Ltd, 182–190 Wairau Road, Auckland 10, New Zealand

Penguin Books Ltd, Registered Offices: Harmondsworth, Middlesex, England

First published in the USA by Pocket Books,
a division of Simon & Schuster, Inc., New York 1990
Published in Penguin Books 1990
3 5 7 9 10 8 6 4

Based upon characters created by David Lynch and Mark Frost
for the television series *Twin Peaks*

Printed in England by Clays Ltd, St Ives plc
Filmset in 10/12½ point Imprint

Dear Diary,   July 22, 1984

My name is Laura Palmer, and as of just three short minutes ago, I officially turned twelve years old! It is July 22, 1984, and I have had such a good day! You were the last gift I opened and I could hardly wait to come upstairs and start to tell you all about myself and my family. You shall be the one I confide in the most. I promise to tell you everything that happens, everything I feel, everything I desire. And, every single thing I think. There are some things I can't tell *anyone*. I promise to tell these things to you.

Anyway, when I came down for breakfast this morning, I saw that Mom had hung streamers all through the house, and even Dad put on a party hat and tooted away on a kazoo for a while. I didn't think Donna and I would ever stop laughing!

Oh, Donna is my very best friend in the whole world. Her last name is Hayward, and her father, Dr Hayward, delivered me twelve years ago today! I can't believe I finally made it. Mom cried at the table because she said before I know it I'll be a grown-up woman. Yeah, sure. It's going to take years for me to even get my period, I just know it. She's crazy if she thinks I'll be grown-up in no time, especially if she keeps giving me stuffed animals for my birthday!

Today was just the way I wanted it to be, with only Donna and Mom and Dad there. And Jupiter, my cat, of course. For breakfast we had apple pancakes, which are my favorite, with lots of maple syrup and sourdough toast.

Donna gave me the blouse I saw in the window at Horne's Department Store, and I know she bought it with her allowances because she was saving all of them for a long time and wouldn't tell me why. It's the most beautiful blouse you've ever seen! It is white and silky and has tiny embroidered roses all over it, but not so many that it looks bad. It's just perfect. On Donna's birthday, I'm going to get her something extra special too.

My cousin Madeline, Maddy for short, is visiting tomorrow for a whole week. She and Donna and I are going to build a fort in the woods and camp out if Mom will let us. I know Dad will. He likes the woods as much as I do. One night I had a dream that Dad moved us to a house deep in the woods and my bedroom had a big tree outside the window with two songbirds nesting there.

I'll be back in a minute, Diary, Dad is calling to me from downstairs. He says he has a surprise! I'll tell you everything when I get back!

Love, Laura

You will never ever believe what just happened! I went downstairs and Dad told Mom and I to get in the car and not to ask any questions until we got to where we were going. Of course, Mom asked questions the whole way. I didn't mind because I thought maybe something would slip out of Dad's mouth, but it didn't. I just kept quiet so that I wouldn't lose my surprise. When we pulled up to The Broken Circle Stables, I knew! Daddy bought me a pony! Diary, he is so beautiful, much more beautiful than I could ever have dreamed. His colors are cinnamon red and deep brown, and his eyes are big and sweet. Mom couldn't believe it when she saw it and started asking Dad how he managed to do it without anyone knowing. Dad said it would ruin the surprise if she knew, and he's right.

Mom nearly had a heart attack when she saw me underneath the pony's legs to find out if it was a boy or a girl. I barely had to look to find out that it was a boy. *Like I've never seen one of those before.* Mom doesn't know her little girl the way she thinks she does, hmmm?

Back to my pony. I decided his name should be Troy, like the pony in Mrs Larkin's photo book. Zippy, who works at the stables, said he would make a nameplate for me that says TROY in big letters, and he'll hang it right in front so that everyone will know his name when they see him. Troy is still too young to ride, but in two months I'll be able to get on and just race through the fields! Today I walked him and fed him carrots (Dad brought them with us in the trunk) and a cube of sugar that Zippy gave me. Troy loved all of it. Before I left him, I whispered in his warm, soft ear that I would see him tomorrow and that I would write all about him, here, in my diary. I can't wait to show him to Donna! I almost forgot, Maddy will see him too!

On the way home from the stables Dad said that Troy and I have the same birthday, because when a pony is given as a gift to someone who will love him, they share everything. So happy birthday to Troy too!

I'm glad I don't know where he came from, because this way, it is almost as if Heaven sent him down just for me.

Anyway, Diary, tomorrow is a big day and tonight I will sleep very well, dreaming of Troy and all of the time we shall spend together. I am the luckiest girl in the world.

Love, Laura

P.S. I hope BOB doesn't come tonight.

Dear Diary, July 23, 1984

It is very late at night and I can't sleep. I have had nightmare after nightmare and have finally chosen to avoid sleeping altogether. I figure Maddy will be tired from her ride out here and will want to take a nap tomorrow anyway, so I can sleep then. Maybe if the sky is light when I sleep, my dreams won't be so dark.

One of them was just awful. I woke up crying, and I was afraid Mom would come in if she heard me, and I just want to be alone right now, and she wouldn't understand that. She always comes in and sings 'Waltzing Matilda' to me when I can't sleep, or like tonight when I have bad dreams. It's not that I don't want her to sing to me, it is just that there was this strange man in my dream singing just that song in Mom's voice, and it frightened me so much I could hardly move.

In the dream I was walking through the woods out by the Pearl Lakes, and there was this very strong wind, but only around me. It was hot. The wind. And about twenty feet away from me there was this man with long hair and very large, callused hands. They were very rough and he held them out to me as he sang. His beard didn't blow in the wind because the wind was only around me. The tips of his thumbs were black like coal and he wiggled them around in circles as his hands got closer to me. I kept walking toward him, even though I didn't want to at all because he frightened me so much.

He said, 'I have your cat,' and Jupiter ran behind him and off into the woods like a little white speck on a piece of black paper. He just kept singing and I tried to tell him I wanted to go home and I wanted Jupiter to come with me, but I couldn't talk. Then he lifted

5

his hands up in the air very, very high, like he was growing bigger and taller every minute, and as his hands went up, I felt the wind around me stop and everything went silent. I thought that he was letting me go because he could read my mind, at least it felt that way. And so when he stopped the wind with his hands like that, I thought he was letting me free, letting me go home.

Then I had to look down because there was this heat between my legs, not nice warm, but hot. It burned me and so I had to spread my legs open so they would cool. So that they would stop burning, so so hot. And they started spreading by themselves like they were going to snap off of my body, and I thought, I'm going to die this way, and how will anyone understand that I tried to keep my legs closed, but they burned and I couldn't. And then the man looked at me and smiled this awful smile, and in Mom's voice he sang, 'You'll come a'waltzing Matilda with me . . .' And I tried to talk again but I couldn't, and I tried to move but I couldn't do that either, and he said, '*Laura, you are home.*' And I woke up.

Sometimes when I'm dreaming I feel trapped there and so frightened. But now when I look at what I just wrote, it doesn't seem so scary. Maybe I'll write down all of my dreams from now on so that I won't have to be afraid of them.

One night last year I had such an awful dream that the whole next day in school, I couldn't work. Donna thought I was going nuts because every time she said my name or touched my shoulder in class to pass a note, I jumped. I wasn't going nuts, like Nadine Hurley or anything, but I was still feeling like I was in a dream. I don't really remember it, but all I know was in the dream I was in a lot of trouble because I hadn't passed this weird test where you have to help a certain number of people across this river in a boat, and I couldn't do it, because I just wanted to swim or something, and so they sent someone after me, to touch me in bad, mean ways. I don't remember any more, and I guess it's no loss.

I'm so tired of waiting to grow up. Some day it will happen and I'll be the only person who can make me feel bad or good about anything I do.

I'll talk to you tomorrow. I'm getting pretty tired.

Laura

Cousin Maddy will be here any minute. Dad went to pick her up at the station by himself because Mom wouldn't let him wake me. I slept until just fifteen minutes ago. No dreams at all, except Mom says she heard me calling out to her and then I hooted like an owl! I'm so embarrassed. She said she came into my room and I was half asleep but I . . . hooted again, and then she says I giggled and rolled over and went back to sleep. I hope she doesn't tell anyone about this. She always tells people things like that when we have dinner parties with the Haywards or something. It always starts with, 'Laura did the sweetest, most odd thing . . .' And I know it's coming.

Like one night she said, right in front of everyone, that I had sleptwalked into the kitchen one night just before she was going to bed. I took off all my clothes, stuffed them in the stove, and went back to bed. Now every time I go to the stove at the Haywards' when Donna and I help with dinner, Mrs Hayward makes a joke about whether or not I realize that the stove is a stove and not a washing machine.

Mom had been drinking the night she told that, so I forgave her. But if she tells anyone I hooted, I'll just die. I don't suppose there is ever a time that parents stop being a source of constant embarrassment to their children. Mine are no exception.

Maybe if I could stop doing stupid things in my sleep, she wouldn't have anything to tell people.

More later.

Laura
(hoot, hoot)

Dear Diary,   July 27, 1984

I have so much to tell you. These words come to
you from the inside of a fort that Donna and Maddy
and I built. Dad and Mom said it was okay as long as
we stayed just out back. We used wood that Ed Hurley
gave us, and Dad hammered everything together.
Donna says that if a storm came up, it would all be
over for us, but I have a feeling it would stand, no
matter what happened.

Maddy is so pretty now. She's sixteen years old and
I'm so jealous of her life! I wish I were sixteen! She
has a boyfriend at home that she already misses, and
he called her at the house earlier just to make sure she
got here all right. Dad teased her about how cutesy she
was on the phone, but Maddy didn't mind. Donna
thinks that when she has a steady boyfriend, she'll
probably be forty years old and going deaf. I told her
she was crazy because boys already like both of us,
we're just too smart to go out with them. I wonder
what it will be like when someone besides my parents
loves me, and if he will call when I travel to make sure
that I'm all right.

Anyway, earlier we all went to see Troy at the
stables and brushed and fed him. Both Donna and
Maddy said they'd never seen such a beautiful pony in
their lives. I wonder what I did to deserve him. Donna
had been wishing for a pony for years too, and her
father never bought her one. I wonder how long Troy
will live and if I will cry for ever when he dies.

Donna just saw what I wrote about Troy's dying,
and she says I think too many sad thoughts, and that
if I keep it up, who knows what will happen. Donna
doesn't know everything I know. I can't help but

think sad thoughts sometimes. Sometimes they are the closest things to my mind.

Mom packed us sandwiches and two thermoses. One filled with milk, ice-cold. The other with hot chocolate. Maddy won't drink more than one cup of the hot chocolate 'cause she says it gives her zits. I don't see a zit on her face anywhere. She started her period three years ago and says it's just a nightmare. It gives you acne and cramps and you're tired and angry all the time you have it. Great. Something else to look forward to. Mom got her period when she was my age, and I only hope that doesn't mean I'll get mine this year too. Now that Maddy has described it to me, I'm not at all interested.

All of us are eating sandwiches and drinking milk, and writing in our diaries. Maddy's is so big and full! Donna's is more full than mine, but I'm going to make you bigger than Maddy's is. I like the idea of keeping my thoughts all in one place, like a brain you can look into. We hung a flashlight from the top of the fort so that the light comes down and we can all see. A little bit of light came from the house windows, but we covered it up because we all agreed that it ruined the feeling of being out in the woods alone. All of the blankets and food already make us feel like we're exactly where we are. In the backyard! Maddy says she brought a pack of cigarettes with her and that later, after Mom and Dad are asleep, if we want to, we can try one. She says they're stale because she's had them for months but hasn't touched them because she's afraid her parents will find out. Maybe I'll try one. Donna says she doesn't want to, and Maddy and I said we wouldn't pressure her because real friends don't do that. But I'll bet you I can make Donna smoke one just by giving her the right look. I just bet you.

More later.

I'm back.

We've been laughing so hard all of our stomachs ache from it. Maddy was describing how she kisses her boyfriend with her tongue, and it made Donna and me crazy. Donna made a face and said she didn't like the idea of tongue-kissing, and I pretended to think the same . . . but honestly, Diary, when I heard how you do it, I got a very strange funny feeling in my stomach. Different from . . . never mind. I got the feeling that I might like tongue-kissing and I'm going to try it with a boy I like as soon as I can. Maddy said she was afraid at first, but she's been doing it for a year now and she loves it. I told both of them about last month when I had a fever and went into my parents' bedroom and saw them naked with Dad on top. I just left the room and Mom came to see me a few minutes later with some aspirin and 7-Up. She never said a word about it. Donna says they were definitely having sex, and I already knew that, but they didn't seem to like it. They just seemed to be moving very slowly and not even really looking at each other.

Maddy thinks it was probably 'just a quickie'. Ugghh. My parents having sex. What a gross thing. I know that's where I came from, but I don't care if I never see that again. I'm promising right now that if and when I ever have sex, it will be a lot more fun than that.

Well, Mom and Dad just came to say goodnight to us, and to tell Donna that her parents called and said she didn't have to go to church tomorrow so that she can sleep in with us. We were all glad to hear that.

Dad made us all close our eyes and open our hands, and he stuck a candy bar in each of them and told us not to tell Mom. Then Mom came in and handed me a little bag and said don't tell your father. There were three more candy bars in the bag! Maddy just looked at her candy and sighed. 'Zits,' was all she could say. But she tore both of them open and we all forced both candy bars into our mouths and tried to sing 'Row, Row, Row Your Boat' while our mouths were full. Donna said the chewed candy looked like something Troy would leave for us, and we all had to spit it out.

Maddy told a pretty good story, a scary one, about a family that goes away for the night and comes home to find people hiding in their house waiting to kill them all. There was more to it than that, but I'm not sure how much I want to remember about it later on. I don't want to feed my dreams. Donna got out of the fort to pee, and Maddy told me that she had been having some bad dreams too. She said she didn't want to talk about them in front of Donna because maybe she wouldn't understand. She says she's been having dreams of me in the woods. Donna came back and Maddy wouldn't say any more. *I wonder if Maddy has seen the long-haired man? Or the wind?* Maddy writes poems in her diary because she says that they are sometimes more fun to write than just the old boring stuff, and just in case anyone ever saw your diary, they might not understand everything if it was in poems. I'll try that tomorrow.

More later.

Aha! I told you I could get Donna to try a cigarette.

12

Maddy brought them out and lit one of them, then she passed it to me to try. I like blowing smoke out of my mouth. Sort of like a spirit coming out of me, a dancing, flowing, wispy spirit. Like I was a grown-up woman with people all around me, just staring like they wanted to be me. Even Donna said I looked like a mature person when I smoked. I didn't even inhale so I wonder what it would be like if I did.

Donna was next, and before she could say no, I just said, 'I'm glad I tried it, and I don't ever have to do it again if I don't want to.' So she took it and made a few puffs of smoke in the fort. She looked good smoking too, but she got kind of scared and sucked some smoke in and started coughing really loud, so we put out the cigarette and aired out the fort real quick in case Mom and Dad woke up. I think I'll buy a pack of cigarettes some day and just keep them like Maddy does. I'm not going to get hooked or anything. I'm too careful.

Well, we're going to bed now and all of us are signing off to our diaries. Good night to you. I think you and I shall be wonderful companions.

Love, Laura

Dear Diary,

Here is a poem.

From the light in my window he can see into me
But I cannot see him until he is close
Breathing, with a smile at my window
He comes to take me
Turn me round and round
Come out and play   Come play
Lie still   Lie still   Lie still.

Little rhymes and little songs
Pieces of the forest in my hair and clothes
Sometimes I see him near me
when I know he can't be there
Sometimes I feel him near me
and I know it is something just to bear.

When I call out
No one can hear me
When I whisper, he thinks the message
Is for him only.
My little voice inside my throat
I always think there must be something
That I've done
Or something I can do
But no one no one comes to help,
He says,
A little girl like you.

Maddy brought a bunch of clothes with her, and she had me try all of them on in front of the mirror. She could tell I was feeling depressed about something . . . I guess. Some of her clothes are very beautiful. I liked the way they made me feel. Especially the short skirt and the high heels with this little fluffy white sweater.

Maddy said I looked like Audrey Horne. She's the daughter of the man, Benjamin Horne, that my father works for. Benjamin is very very very rich. Audrey is a pretty girl but she's quiet and sometimes mean. Her father doesn't pay much attention to her, and that's probably why she acts that way. He has been very attentive to me, however, all of my life. Each time there is a party or a get-together at the Great Northern, Benjamin puts me on his lap or knee and sings to me softly in my ear. Sometimes I feel very bad for Audrey, because when she sees him singing to me, it must make her sad because she often runs from the room and doesn't come back until her mother makes her. Other times I kind of feel good when she runs off. Like I am the center of attention, and that I am more special to him than his own daughter. I know that isn't nice to say, but I'm just being honest.

To be very honest, I think I like the way I looked in Maddy's clothes too. Something stirred inside me like a bubble. The way you feel on a carousel when you're not used to the up and down of it yet. I'll bet if I dressed this way all the time, things would be very different.

Maddy and I took a walk later on, but of course, in our jeans and T-shirts. Twin Peaks doesn't see many high heels and short skirts without banners all around announcing a dance or festival. We walked to Easter Park and sat in the gazebo for a while. Maddy said that her life at home is fine, 'except for the sometimes unbelievable nosiness of my parents'. I made sure to quote her exactly there because I thought it was so well put. She said that there are a lot of things in life, she thinks, that don't seem right at first, and then you settle into them.

Maybe that's how I should start thinking. Maybe I should be a better person and not think so much all the time about what is happening to me. I hope some day soon I'll be good enough at this to rid myself of all the things that trouble me so. Things I still cannot even describe other than in bits and pieces. If I am a better person, and if I try harder every day, perhaps all of this will work out.

Love, Laura

SOME DAY GROWING UP WILL COME EASIER

Deep inside are woman's hills about to come up
To see the sky
To see the sun and moon
And the tiny stars in the black of a man's hand

Sometimes in the morning
I'll look across myself
See hills and valleys forming
Think of rivers underground.

Outside me
I am blooming
Inside I am dry

If only I could understand
The reason for my crying
If only I could stop this fear
Of dreaming that I'm dying.

I haven't written for a long time, and for that I am truly sorry. Maddy left three days ago, and I feel very frightened inside about something I do not understand.

One good thing happened. In the middle of the night last night, I had the most wonderful sensation inside me. Like something warm in my chest, and warm between my legs. My whole body went inside out, it seemed, and I felt like I could just float away. *I think I had one of those orgasms* in my sleep. It's so awful and so embarrassing to write, but kind of nice at the same time.

Right after it, I had this fantasy that a boy came into my room and put his hand across my nightgown and touched me softly. He whispered nice, gentle things, and then said I had to lie very still or he would leave. Then he pulled me to the end of the bed by my feet, and when my knees were bent over the end of my mattress, he made me close my eyes and I felt him open me up, bigger and bigger, and I had to look to see what was happening, and when I did, he was gone. But I looked at my stomach and I was pregnant. He was inside me, but small like a baby. I wish it hadn't ended like that. I don't know why my brain did that. I like it better when he was pulling me down gently and taking soft control.

                                                    Laura

I spent the afternoon with Troy today, cleaning him, and brushing and feeding him. I was fascinated by how much he seems to understand how I'm feeling. He nuzzled up against me for a long time while I brushed his mane and head, and when I sat down in the corner of his stall, he lowered his head, and I let him breathe all across my neck and face. I wonder if people fall deeply in love with horses the way I love mine, or if I am wrong to be thinking or feeling any of these things.

I wish Donna were here. I really wish Maddy were here. I'm going to call Donna and see if she can come over for a sleepover or something. Maybe I could go there. That might even be better. Sometimes my bedroom is the best place in the world, and other times it is like a place that closes in and suffocates me.

I wonder if it's like that when you die . . . suffocating. Or if it's like they say it is when you're in church. That you float up and up until Jesus sees you and takes your hand. I'm not sure I want to be near Jesus when I die. I might make a mistake, even just a small one, and upset him. I don't know enough about him to know what might make him mad. Sure, the Bible says he's forgiving and has died for my sins and loves everyone no matter their faults . . . but people say I am the perfect daughter, the happiest girl in the world, and one without any troubles. *And that is not true at all.* So how will I know if Jesus is really like me? Scared and bad sometimes even though most people might not know how and when? I'll probably be a gift to Satan, if I am not careful. Sometimes when I have to see BOB, I think I am with Satan anyway, and that

I'll never make it out of the woods in time to be Laura, good and true and pure, ever again.

Sometimes I think that life would be so much easier if we didn't have to think about being boys or girls or men or women or old or young, fat or thin . . . if we could all just be certain we were the same. We might be bored, but the danger of life and of living would be gone . . .

I'll be back after I call Donna.

Donna said she wishes we could do something together tonight, but her family is having 'family night' tonight. I guess it's just me and you, Diary. Maybe we can go out to the woods soon and smoke one of the cigarettes Maddy left for me. There are four of them, and I hid them carefully in the bedpost. That's where I hide notes from school I don't want Mom to find when she's in here cleaning/snooping – you know, mom stuff. I love her, but she doesn't always understand what I try to tell her. She'd probably have a heart attack if she knew all of the things that go on in my head. Anyway, the knob comes off and there is a hole there. Dad would call it a 'cavity'. It is about four inches deep and it is the perfect hiding place. You can't even tell the knob comes off as long as there is a purse strap or sweater over the post.

So maybe we can go out, just you and I, with a flashlight and a cigarette and just talk to each other. I know you, more than even Donna, can keep a secret. I could never tell Mom about the sexy stuff I think about. I'm afraid that if I let it come out of my mouth that God will hear, or that someone will know how bad I am, and they'll say . . . *Nobody else ever thinks things like that!*

I'll bet they don't. I'll bet I'll never get the man I want, because any time we try to kiss or fool around, he'll think I'm a crazy person who is sick and weird. I hope I'm not. I would be so awfully sad if that were true. How could I stop thinking the way that I do? I can't stop my mind from wanting to think things like that. The thoughts that make my body warm, and my chest go up and down, filling with air and letting go, the way they do in books and movies, but still different, because they never talk about the fantasies I have.

I'm going to go downstairs for dinner now. I wish I could fit you in the bedpost too. For now I will tape you to the wall behind my bulletin board. I hope you won't fall!

More later, Laura

Here we are. About a mile from home, just before
dark. The summer months seem to make the woods
less dangerous until later at night. It is warm out, and
you and I are sitting together leaning at the base of a
great tree. A Douglas fir. Donna's and my favorite.
When I look up, it is like the tree is cradling me.

I think I'll smoke that cigarette. I brought a soda
just so I could put the ashes and the butt in the can so
as not to set the whole town of T.P. on fire. We call
Twin Peaks T.P. in school sometimes. The world
wipes its butt with T.P. Bobby Briggs says that the
most. Then he pulls all the girls' hair and makes
burping noises in our faces. He likes us all, of course. I
was in the Double R. one day after school and he came
in just after me and tugged on my hair super hard.

Norma winked at me and asked if we had set the
date for the wedding yet. She's off her rocker if she
thinks I go near him. Any boy I go near won't be
pulling on my hair like that ... I think he'd pull on
my hair the way they do in my fantasies. With their
whole hand, slowly making a fist at the back of my
head, and pulling me close for a tongue kiss.

I wonder if all penises look the way Dad's does. I
can still see Mom trying to cover it with the sheet that
night. It sort of reminded me of something raw. Something that might be okay in a while, or was okay a
while ago, before someone pulled all of the skin off it
and got it looking all pink and weird. Maybe I'll see a
nicer one some day. God, I hope I do. I won't lie there
like Mom did. Just like a fish on the dock, trying to
learn how to breathe out of water. Little tiny huffs and
puffs, but nothing else. If I can find the right man,

maybe I'll be comfortable enough to act just the way I think girls should when they are with someone. Half in control and half . . . I don't know the word. Maybe I'm getting too nasty. I would just die if anyone saw what I've written.

The owls have started hooting. One of them is just above me in the tree . . . Something about him is strange. I know it is a boy owl, and I feel like he's watching me. Each time I look up at him his head moves like he is quickly turning away from me. I wonder if he knows what I've been writing. God, I had better start being a very good girl. Right away. Perhaps he is a bird like in that story I read. This big bird could swoop down and rest on someone's shoulder, acting very sweet, but would then read the person's mind. If the person was thinking bad thoughts, the bird would peck away at the person's eyes and ears so that there would only be questions of sound and sight in the person's head, instead of bad and nasty thoughts.

I dream of flying sometimes. I wonder if birds dream of going to school or to work sometimes. Having suits and dresses instead of the feathers we dream of. I would fly right over Twin Peaks and out over the land beyond it. I'd never come back if I didn't have to.

I'll write a poem, then head back home.

> Inside me there is something
> No one knows about
> Like a secret
> Sometimes it takes over
> And I drift back
> Deep into darkness.
> This secret tells me

I will never grow older
Never laugh with friends
Never be who I should if I ever reveal
Its name.

I cannot tell if it is real
Or if I dream of it
For when it touches me
I drift off
No tears come
No screams
I am wrapped up
In a nightmare of hands
And of fingers
And of small tiny voices in the woods.
So wrong
So beautiful
So bad
So Laura.

I have to go home. Now. It is too dark. This is not a
nice place to be right now.

Laura

Dear Diary,   August 16, 1984

Never before in my life have I been so confused. It is five-thirty exactly in the morning, and I can barely hold this pen I am shaking so much. I have been in the woods again. Lost. But have been led. I think I am a very bad person. Tomorrow I will start a new way of living. I will not think any more bad thoughts. I will not think any more about sex. Maybe he will stop coming if I try harder to be good. Maybe I could be like Donna. She is a good person. I am bad.

                                                            Laura

P.S. I promise, I promise, I promise to be good!

Dear Diary,   August 31, 1984

I have not written to you for ages because I have been trying so hard to be happy and good and around people all the time so that I am never alone to think about the wrong things. Today I must write to you, though, to tell you of the news.

I got my period. It is not all what I thought it would be. School starts next week and now this. I was getting out of bed this morning and saw the blood. I called for Mom, and she of course made this enormous deal out of the whole thing. She called Dad when I had told her not to tell anyone. And now everyone probably knows up at the Great Northern. All I wanted was some damn pads or something, and she has to go into all of this stuff about how I am now a woman and everything. Okay. Okay. So it is kind of special. But this can only make things worse if I am not careful. I'm in bed now with cramps.

Mom moved the television into my room, which was nice, and I have a heating pad on my belly and tons of aspirin on my nightstand. Television doesn't interest me much, so I am left once again with strange thoughts of life and of . . . other things. I guess what is coming from me was to be the life source of some other being. I am glad there is no one inside me right now. At least not a child.

Sometimes I think there is someone inside me, but it is another, stranger part of me. *Sometimes I see her in the mirror*. I don't know that I ever want to have children of my own. Something happens to parents, or people who become parents. I think they forget they were ever children themselves and that things might embarrass or upset their kids sometimes, but they

have just forgotten or decided to ignore that. Too
many bad things happen to me sometimes late at
night, so I probably would not be such a good mother.
This makes me sad inside.

I am glad of one thing. Jupiter is beside me in bed,
and he is purring away softly. Like you, he would
never criticize me.

Laura

September 1, 1984

My breasts ache, which is almost silly because they're so tiny. I'll admit they are bigger than they were last week, and certainly nicer looking. Always hard at the little pink tips. But God they hurt.

Mom came in earlier and we actually had a nice talk. I told her I wished she hadn't told Dad about my period, and she apologized but said she only did it because she knew how proud he would be of his little girl's becoming a woman. She changed the water in my heating pad and rubbed my stomach for a long time. We didn't need to say anything to each other for a long while, and still I felt like we were talking.

'She crawled into bed with me for about an hour after that and let me fall asleep on her shoulder. We shared a soda when I woke up, and for the first time in a long while, I felt like we were really close.

I hope I can sleep through the night tonight.

Love, Laura

Dear Diary,   September 9, 1984

I have discovered something about myself. Do you remember the night I told you I woke up with that wonderful feeling? Well! There is a special place on my body that lets me feel that as often as I like. A warm, wonderful place where everything else melts away and I am free to just feel good. My little secret red button. This is all mine. Finally something that will take me away along with my fantasies. I can do it in my bed, very softly with my fingertip, which is so sweet. I can do it in the bathtub with the water as it pours out of the faucet. (I never knew a bath could be so enjoyable!) Or in the shower, with a small stream of water coming from above. I move and jump and sometimes have to grab a pillow and put it over my head so that it is dark and no one can hear me making little noises. It is, after all, a secret, and whether this is right or wrong, I feel very good when it happens and no one need ever know, except you, dear Diary.

It has been quite a week with my period coming and all, and now this sweet-as-honey discovery. Now I am beginning to feel like a woman, and some day very soon, perhaps, I will share this with someone special.

Good night! Good night! Good night!

Laura

P.S. I hope in my heart that I am not doing something that is wrong by touching myself. I hope this is something all girls do, and that I won't be punished for it later.

To the person invading my privacy:September 15, 1984

I cannot believe the distrust I feel in my family and friends. I know for a fact that my diary was taken and read by someone, maybe several someones. I will not be writing any more in this diary for a long time, if ever. You have ruined my trust and my feeling of security. I hate you for that, whoever you are!

On these pages I have written things sometimes too scary or too embarrassing even to read again myself . . . I trust that these pages are turned only by me, only when I wish. Many things are hurting and confusing me. I need my private pages, in order to see my mind outside me, push it away.

Please stay away from this diary.
I mean it.

Laura

Dear Diary, October 3, 1985

I have decided, over twelve months later, to begin speaking to you again. I have found a hiding place I will not speak of, in case you are found outside it and someone nosy wishes to know of its whereabouts.

I know it was not your fault someone found you and decided to pry, but it has taken me a long time to feel safe enough to write in your pages again. Many, many things have happened since you last heard from me, and many of these things have proven that my thoughts on the world's being mostly a cruel and sad place are true and have been confirmed as such.

I trust no one, and only rarely myself. I struggle most mornings, afternoons, and evenings with what is right and what is wrong. I do not understand if I am being punished for something I have done wrong, something I don't remember, or if this happens to everyone, and I am just too stupid to understand it.

First of all, I found out that Dad did not give Troy to me. Benjamin Horne did. The details are not important, but let's just say I overheard Audrey arguing with her dad about it, when I was up at the Great Northern visiting Johnny. Johnny is Audrey's brother, Benjamin's other child. Johnny is slow. He is older than I am, but has the mentality of a young child. That's what the doctors say at least.

Sometimes I think he's just chosen to keep quiet because it is so much more interesting sometimes to just listen to people instead of talking to them. He never speaks except to say 'Yes' or 'Indian'. He loves Indians. He wears a headdress constantly. One made of beautifully colored feathers and dyed strips of leather. In his eyes the world is a strange mix of

31

happiness and pain, and I think I understand Johnny more than I do a lot of other people. Perhaps I could find a way to spend more time with him. He is so often left alone.

I am glad that Troy is my pony, and I love riding him, walking with him, and just watching him graze. But now I feel awkward about Dad. Like he is less of an honest man for claiming that Troy was a gift from him. Maybe Benjamin wanted it that way, I don't know. But no matter what, I am somehow more intrigued by Benjamin now and feel like I owe him more than Dad.

Sometimes I think that I would rather not have gotten a pony of my own at all, because that way I wouldn't have lost any respect for Dad, and Benjamin would just have been Benjamin. Even worse, Audrey and I will probably never ever get along now. I am a little sick inside that I am the one who caused this. Also it gives me a feeling of power. Why do these things happen to me?

You know, I think out of all the men I know in the world, Dr Hayward has been the most loving to me. He is unselfish, kind, and always shows me a gentle smile of inspiration or forgiveness – or anything that somehow always perfectly fills the gap I feel inside me. Thirteen years ago, he brought me into the world and held tight to my small body, for just a moment. In daydreams, I imagine that moment to be one of the warmest there ever was in my life. I love him for holding me, that frightened young child fresh to the air and light, and for making me believe, without even a word, that he would hold me again if I ever needed him to.

He reminds me of someone I wouldn't mind seeing every day of my life. A grandfather sweetness, inside a father's helping hand.

I'll be back after dinner. There is plenty of more news.

Love, Laura

Dear Diary,   October 3, 1985, later

Dinner was good tonight. One of my favorite meals, potato pancakes with creamed-corn topping and vegetables on the side. I'll have to start changing the way I eat soon, or run the risk of blowing up like a balloon. Mom made it special for me tonight because she knows I'm still upset about Jupiter. She and Dad ate chicken instead.

Jupiter is the other news. Usually he'll go out back and play in the yard area. It isn't fenced in, but he never wandered. I guess he was too smart to leave a home that loved him so much and fed him so well. Even though I didn't write to you often of him, he was one of the most special things in the world to me, always sweet and gentle. Always loved me no matter what I looked like or what I had done wrong or right for the day.

Often, on nights that I could not sleep, the two of us would play downstairs with a ball of string, to only the light of the tiny wall lamp. We would enjoy ice cream in the kitchen afterward. He was a true vanilla fan. It would be dark in the house, and the two of us prowled together until sleep found us, hours after we had given up on getting any at all. I still have a photo Dad took of Jupiter and me on the living room couch after one of these nights. We hadn't made it back upstairs to sleep and had fallen asleep on the couch instead.

I gave the photo of Jupiter to Sheriff Truman so that he could post it in the station. I hope they find whoever hit Jupiter. I know it was probably an accident, because a few minutes before it happened, he had found a small mouse or something ... I hadn't paid much attention, but he raced off with it and was hit out on the road. Mom heard the noise and called for me to stay where I was until she knew what had happened. But sometimes Mom and I think the same thoughts, have the same dreams, and she knows better than to think I'd stay in my room *when I knew*. So I didn't listen and went out to see him, still breathing for a few moments afterward, and bleeding from his eyes and tummy.

I can't believe someone could hit a cat like that, right in the middle of the day, and not tell someone. Not think to stop and come to the closest house and report what had happened. Mom heard the car screech, and Dad says he wishes he had been home because he might have been able to tell what kind of car it was that hit him, just by the sound. I doubt it, but it was a nice thought.

He's buried outside now. A good friend gone, when I so cherish the few I have. I wish something else would have died instead of Jupiter.

To be honest with you, as I always am, many people in Twin Peaks like me. Lots know my name, and especially at school I feel quite popular. The only problem is that I don't really know any of these people the way they think they know me. And I think I am safe in saying, they don't know me at all. Donna knows the most.

But still I am afraid to tell her of my fantasies and my nightmares, because sometimes she is good at understanding, and other times she just giggles, and I don't have the nerve to ask why things like that are funny to her. So I feel badly again and shut up about it for a long time. I love Donna very much, but sometimes I worry that she wouldn't be around me at all if she knew what my insides were like. Black and dark, and soaked with dreams of big, big men and different ways they might hold me and take me into their control. A fairy princess who thinks she has been rescued from the tower, but finds that the man who takes her away is not there to save her, but instead to go inside her, deep. To ride her as if she were an animal, to tease her and make her close her eyes, and listen as he tells her all that he does. Step by step. I hope that is not a bad thing to think.

Love, Laura

Dear Diary,   October 12, 1985

I tried a marijuana cigarette the other night. Donna and I had a sleepover at her place, but her parents went out for the night with mine to the Great Northern for a party Benjamin was throwing. Donna and I didn't really want to go, and I especially didn't because of Audrey. I talked Donna into riding our bikes up to the Book House to meet some new people. It took me for ever to convince her I wouldn't tell anyone, and that we would be back before our parents. Finally she agreed because both of us have been terribly bored with all the same faces around all the time.

We were barely there a half hour before these guys, Josh and Tim, and one other one, but I can't remember his name, came up to us. I was smoking a cigarette that I stole from the reception desk at the Great Northern one day when I brought Johnny an Indian storybook.

They thought we were older because one of us was smoking. So Josh came up with Tim and the other guy. They said they were from Canada, and there was no doubt about that because they couldn't stop saying 'ay'. 'Want a better cigarette, ay?' Tim liked Donna right away, which freaked her out a little because all three of them were like twenty years old. None of them rocked my boat. They all looked like nice guys. I felt pretty safe, but not excited . . . you know what I mean?

Anyway, I said I wanted to try a better cigarette, and Donna and I followed them out to the back of the Book House to do it. Donna made up this elaborate story about how we were just visiting Twin Peaks for the night, and that we had to meet our tour bus in less than an hour. She said we were on a tour called 'Round About the Woods'. I guess they believed her because they hurried up and lit this thing right up. Josh said we might not feel it the first time, but Donna and I proved him wrong. He said we had to 'Hold it in, ay?' And we did . . . six times! Diary, it was amazing. Talk about feeling relaxed and warm and a little bit . . . sexy.

I called Donna 'Trisha', and she called me 'Bernice'! (Just in case they ever came back and asked for us . . . for any reason. We didn't want anyone to know.) So, we were absolutely laughing harder than I ever have before. Every single thing I saw was hysterical. Everything was blurred and kinda wavy, like I was looking at the world through the bottom of an empty water glass. There was a warm, summer wind, and the trees smelled so good.

Tim brought us a cup of coffee with chocolate mixed in, and all five of us sat and talked about all sorts of things, like if maybe our universe was just a tiny little speck of lint that a huge giant hadn't noticed on his sweater, and some day soon, who knows if this great giant would just brush us off, or toss us into a washer and drown us all to death. Donna said maybe our idea of hundreds of years is only a split second to this giant, and soon something would have to happen, because how long can someone keep a sweater on?

We all liked the idea that there might be other little universes or 'balls of lint' on this sweater, and we thought we'd some day like to meet a few people from these other places, as long as they were nice to us. We could hear a little bit of music coming out of the Road House, and I just had to get up and dance a little. I felt better than I had in ages, just floating in the night air and feeling warm inside.

Donna even danced with me for a few minutes until she realized we had to go meet ... OUR TOUR BUS! We had to lie and say we rented the bikes from the lost-and-found at the sheriff's station, but I don't think the guys bought that story at all. They were nice not to say anything to us about it, if they did know. Maybe it added excitement to their night, too. Then again, maybe not, because they're older and have probably had much more exciting nights than that.

When we were riding home, we kept having to stop because we had such giggles. Then I got the most outrageous craving for cookies and milk, like I'd die if I didn't have any, and Donna agreed a hundred per cent that we had to have something sweet. She said there was pie at her house, but that didn't seem right. So we emptied our pockets and went into the Cash and Carry for treats. We bought so much junk that we had to walk our bikes back to Donna's house so that we could each hold a bag. All the way home we were paranoid just like the guys said we would be because our eyes were all bloodshot and we wanted to get home before our parents did.

We totally lucked out because just when we got into the house, Dr Hayward called and said they were going to be a bit longer because Benjamin was showing slides or something. Thank God! We ran upstairs and put eye drops in our eyes, then turned on the stereo and ate and danced and laughed, and we were totally sound asleep when everyone got back.

I know drugs are bad, but I'm beginning to get the feeling I like being that way. Kind of bad.

More tomorrow, Laura

It is a little over one week later and I have more
news. Sorry I haven't written, but it has really been
kind of crazy around here ... well, here inside me, at
least. Home is just the same. Irritating more than
anything else. God, I feel so trapped sometimes, like I
have to wear this permanent grin on my face or else
everyone freaks out on me.

I wonder if pain, the kind that doesn't just happen
when your cat is killed, or when an aunt dies, but the
kind that you have to live with ... can it ever be a
friend? Pain as a shadow or companion. I wonder if
that's possible ...

Anyway, the news is strange. I'm a little nervous
about how much I've enjoyed the danger of it all, but
I'll tell you everything and get it off my chest. Maybe
it will be like my dreams, less difficult to understand if
I see it on paper. Here goes.

Last Friday, the day before yesterday, Donna and I
went back to the Book House at about four in the
afternoon. I guess we went back hoping Josh and Tim
and their friend would be there again, and we could
get high on another funny cigarette. We got sort of
dressed up, not too dressy or crazy because we do
know *everyone* in town practically and we didn't want
it to get back to our parents. But we had on skirts that
were pretty short and a little tighter than most people
would approve of, except boys, of course, and we
played with some make-up that Donna's mom, Mrs
Hayward, had given her as an Easter present because
Donna wanted to try some and her mom wanted her to
have her own.

Anyway, again! We got to the Book House and no

one except Big Jake Morrissey was there. He's the guy who runs the place. I guess I should tell you about it so you can imagine where I was. It is a coffee house, mostly for guys – girls are allowed – but it's more like a guy's hangout. There are books everywhere on the tables and shelves, which lined all three walls, all the way to the back. It smells like cigarettes, after-shave, and coffee. There's always coffee brewing. And this time I was inside, I noticed a picture of the man perfect for my fantasies! I didn't say anything, of course, but he's just perfect. Rough and tough, but has puppy-dog eyes and soft skin.

The picture is of him in jeans and a leather jacket, holding a book and sitting on his motorcycle, reading. I am in love! So we were the only ones in the place, and Jake gave us coffee and said that people would be coming in soon, and it might be wise if we left when they started to come in, especially dressed like we were. He was half joking, half serious when he asked us, 'Are you girls looking for trouble of a boy nature?'

Donna turned all red, and I just told him what I would tell Mom or Dad if they ever found out. 'We're just playing around and pretending. It's just for fun, not for trouble.' He understood, or 'bought it', rather, and after we finished our coffee we left. On the way out though, I told Jake that about a week ago, three really nice Canadian boys had been there and had helped Donna and I fix our flat tires after we had run over the broken beer-bottle glass that's always out in front of the Road House. I told him that if he saw them – Josh, Tim, and another guy with blond hair – that he should tell them we wanted to thank them with a cup of coffee, or something. Then I told him we'd

41

probably be out back, just talking, if they showed up. Jake said he'd relay the message if they came in.

You guessed it! They showed up. Jake must have told them what I said because they came out laughing and giving us a hard time for lying to them before. Donna was pretty quick and smart to say that 'we wanted to make sure that you guys were cool before we told you who we were or anything.'

They all said we looked really nice, and I found out the third guy's name was Rick, and all of them are twenty-two! We said our age wasn't important and wouldn't't stop any of us from having fun as long as we were home by ten. If it was going to be later, we would have to call. Josh said he had some alcohol, and if there was a place we knew of to build a small fire or something out in the woods, we could all go out there and have a little party. By this time it was about five-thirty or so.

They were in a truck this time instead of on bikes, and so Donna and I got in the open back and told them to cross Lucky Highway 21 and head into the woods behind Low Town. We both figured it would be safer there, and if anything happened, I could just say that I had gotten lost with Donna, that we had taken a walk or something and lost track of where we were. It would be okay, I figured, no matter what. These guys seemed nice enough, so we trusted them a second time.

We got to a place where there was a stream and hardly any needles on the ground, so the fire would be a safe idea. Tim and Rick looked for kindling while Josh opened up this bottle of . . . I guess it was gin that he had. The only alcohol Donna and I had ever had was a glass of champagne – one glass, at Dr Hayward's birthday party last year. This was brand-new to both of us. Donna seemed excited, but nervous, too. I was just plain excited and was the first to drink a sip of it after Josh. We just passed it around . . . until it was empty.

Donna and I were really messed up almost instantly. Rick kept saying. 'They're toasted, man.'

Both Donna and I had to pee, so we went away from the fire about thirty feet and crouched down behind a tree. For a moment there, we were both scared. Real scared. We didn't know how to act, and both of us kept thinking we were saying stupid things or sounding too young or something.

When I stood up, my head got light. I thought to myself, 'It's too late now, you're already drunk, you better just enjoy it, and don't forget to keep watching the time!' Donna agreed that we had just better go with the flow and stick close together in case we got scared again.

Tim turned on the truck stereo, and I asked if it would be stupid if I danced around for a while, 'cause I liked the song. All three said it was okay, and Donna just sat there staring at the fire for a while. Tim went and sat really close to her and whispered something in her ear. Her eyes got real big and she kinda laughed and then relaxed. I guess he made her feel good or pretty or something. I'll have to remember to ask her what he whispered to her.

So I was dancing, and Josh and Rick couldn't stop watching me . . . and I was feeling pretty comfortable, or confident, or both, but I just went a little bit crazy and got into a sexier dance. One that I practiced alone in my room in front of the mirror. I moved my hips around in circles and let my arms move slow, and sometimes I touched my hips like it felt good to me to touch myself.

Darn! Mom's calling me downstairs to do the dishes. I'll be right back. There's lots more!

Love, Laura

Diary, I'm back. Sorry I had to stop.

So I was dancing, and Donna saw what I was doing and looked at me like I was crazy. She looked around for a minute and I guess she wanted to be a part of the attention, too, or something because she looked at her watch and said, 'Let's go skinny-dipping!'

That right there should tell you how drunk Donna was. Everybody got quiet and just listened to the music for a second, then said, 'Yeah, okay.'

So Donna and I took off our clothes . . . all of them. We almost left our panties on, but we were afraid they would think we were stupid little girls. They were all in the stream sitting against the rocks when we came back to the fire. The stream is probably three and a half feet deep at its deepest place. So they were sitting there and we set our clothes down and stood by the fire for a minute. When we moved toward the water, Josh said, 'Stop. There. Just for a minute.'

So we did. And after a minute of us just waiting, he said to Tim and Rick, 'Have you ever in your life seen such a beautiful sight as these two girls?' They both made noises like they liked it, too. Donna and I kind of moved a little when we realized they were staring at us like that . . . that close, you know? Tim said, 'Look

44

at the way the fire makes shadows on their skin.'
Donna and I looked at each other, then looked back
toward them. They were hard to see because we were
so close to the light and they were in the dark in the
stream. Rick just said, 'Please, please come into the
water with us.' We did.

It was so amazing. The way they felt when we got
close under the water, soft and slippery, was like I was
dreaming. I'd never felt anything so nice and so close
to what I'd fantasized about. All of them had . . . hard
. . . hard . . . I guess I'll call them cocks, because
'penis' sounds like a word you only read in Sex Ed
books. So they were all hard.

And I said (mainly because I knew Donna was more
freaked out than I was by all of this), I said, 'Let's
make tonight a play night . . . we can all go home with
that nice feeling of wishing more had happened . . .?
Donna and I are not going to go all the way with you.'

When it came out of my mouth, I couldn't believe it
for a second. Who was talking? What was I, Laura
Palmer – thirteen years old – doing out here in the
woods like this with three naked boys nine years older
than I am?

They all said okay, but Josh said, 'Can we at least
touch you, and maybe get a kiss?' Donna looked at me
the same way she did a year ago when Maddy was
talking about kissing. I told them I didn't mind, but if
Donna did, they couldn't force her. Something tells
me now, when I look back, that this was probably the
most excited these guys had been, ever. I don't think
they would have done anything bad even if we had
asked for it, because they were just as scared. It was
such a personal and strange night. It was like the

woods got us all acting crazy, like the trees and the fact that it had gotten dark made us forget anything else existed. It was eight-thirty and we only had about an hour until we would have to go back home.

I kneeled down in the stream in front of Josh and got my hair wet. Then, I looked at him and I said, 'You can touch them if you want to. It's okay.' So he was real slow, and he put his hands on my breasts, which have gotten to be a good size, I think, for my age, and he shook for a second, like he was amazed. *I felt like I was on top of the world. I was making this twenty-two-year-old boy go crazy inside!* He touched them, then touched just my nipples, and I had a hard time not saying how good that felt, so I laughed.

Tim started touching Donna's breasts, and she just watched him silently as he did it. Rick didn't have anyone to be with so I said, 'You can touch me, too . . . but remember, we all made a deal . . . right?' He nodded and crawled in the water up to me and put his mouth on my nipple. I had to close my eyes so that they wouldn't come out of my head completely. It felt so incredible! I couldn't help but think of the guy in the photo in the Book House, and even if this sounds weird, I'm going to say it.

I had the sexiest thought that he was nursing on me. Like inside me was all of the warmth and nourishment he would ever need . . . this older boy, needing me. I felt strong and almost like I was making a fantasy for them. Josh put his mouth on my other nipple, and Tim and Donna moved away from us a little in the water and just started talking. Then Donna got out with Tim and got dressed and just sat by the fire . . . talking more. I didn't care, or couldn't care. I wasn't going to stop this until I had to, it felt too good to spoil it.

I whispered to Josh and Rick that I had a wish that one of them would kiss me, real soft and slow . . . and that maybe the other could keep touching me the way they were doing already. Rick said Josh could kiss me, as long as he got one, too, later, or whatever.

So Josh leaned to me and got real close, and just before he was going to kiss me he said, real quite – 'Softly, right?' And I told him yes. And he said, 'Soft and slow . . .' And he opened his mouth, and I opened mine, and our tongues started to move together like we were wanting more and more . . . but it wasn't fast, it was slow . . . so nice and slow. And Rick was sucking on my nipples and making noises like he was hungry and getting fed, or like he was eating an ice cream that was delicious. No matter what he was feeling, believe me, I felt ten times better than he sounded.

I went into a dream for I don't know how long while this was happening, and it was like nothing bad ever happened to me ever. Everything disappeared and I suddenly didn't care if I never saw Donna, Mom, Dad, anyone . . . ever again. This warm feeling of being needed, wanted, and special, like I was a treasure . . . was all I wanted to feel, for ever. I had no age, and there was no time or schoolwork or troubles or chores or anything to cloud my mind or bring me back to little Laura. I was ageless, and I was everything these two boys wanted. I was something from their dreams!

Rick began to kiss me next, and he was just as gentle and sweet, but had a different way of kissing. He moved his tongue and lips differently, and he would stop and bite very softly sometimes on my lips, like a tease.

I know I'm going on and on, Diary, but I have to tell someone, and Donna, even though she was there, really wasn't there the way I was. She wasn't ready for it or for the way it would make her feel. Not that there's anything wrong with it, but Donna is still more interested in being good . . . all the way through. Me, I think that I am being good, as much as I can, and maybe more than most people, but I've needed to forget things for a long time now . . . and this was an incredible solution.

Nothing more than that happened in the stream, except I did touch both of them between the legs. I was soft to them the way they were with me, and I thought it was wonderful that they were so hard, and that their hardness floated in the water . . . something I could only feel and not see. Just the way I wanted it. I was able to want more, but able to enjoy what I had.

Tim and Donna exchanged phone numbers while I was getting dressed, and the only thing I was at all worried about was that I was really drunk and starting to feel a little sick to my stomach. I guess Donna was, too, because Tim said, 'Maybe we should help them throw up or something, so that it doesn't happen when they get home . . . Donna, here, is worried, you know, about how she would explain it to her parents.'

I couldn't believe how cool these guys were being to us. They didn't crack one joke or make us feel like we were nothings next to them. I know we aren't, but it was nice, especially in the state we were in, not to hear anything like that. Rick said there was chewing gum in the truck's glove compartment, and if we wanted some, we could have it. I tried to picture going home the way I was, tipsy and all dazed. Throwing up didn't sound like fun, but Tim suggested it might help sober us up, so Donna and I went off and stuck our fingers down our throats. Up it came. It was awful, but I did feel better, and Donna said it was easier for her to walk after that. I said we should probably get going, and that if they didn't mind, maybe they could drop us like a block from home, either house? I thought the truck ride, and the fresh air, would help, too.

Hang on a second, Diary – Mom wants a kiss good night.

Okay, I'm back. Thank God she didn't see you.

When the boys dropped us off, we hopped out of the back, and Tim kissed Donna's hand really romantically, and Rick and Josh said they really enjoyed meeting her. I went to the driver's window, where Josh was, and I was about to thank him ... and I guess just say whatever came out ... but he stopped me. (A chill ran down my back.) He put his finger over my lips and said, 'I don't think I'll ever forget you, Laura.' And he smiled and Rick said, 'Thanks for trusting us the way you did.' They drove off, and Donna and I almost cried.

We were a block from Donna's house and we each put an extra piece of gum in our mouths and rehearsed our story. *We were in the woods, just talking. We were making up stories and talking about dreams we had, and ... the future.*

Donna said she didn't feel like she was lying because that's what she and Tim did do. They kissed a couple of times, and Donna admitted, right before we walked into her house, that she really liked it.

I decided we shouldn't explain anything we did while we were out, unless someone asked. I've seen people overexplain things and it makes it seem like they're lying or hiding something, which we would be.

Donna's parents were asleep on the couch when we walked in, and we snuck past them and up to Donna's room. We brushed our teeth and fixed our hair a little, and before we went downstairs, we hugged each other. We didn't say a word. We just hugged. I think it was our way of saying that it was our secret, and that we were still friends, and that we were okay. *We were home, and we were okay.*

Donna woke her dad up and said we'd been waiting to wake him because he looked so peaceful, sleeping there leaning his head on Mrs Hayward's shoulder. He offered to drive me home, so I called Mom, and she said she hadn't even realized the time because she was reading a really good book. She said Dad was already in bed. She said she'd wait up for me.

I didn't feel guilty about what happened, but I think that's only because no one was worried, and the boys were so nice. I just can't help but get sad inside when I realize that it's over. That night is gone, and I'm Laura again. Thirteen years old, and the apple of my daddy's eye. Not with anger, but with anticipation, I look forward to being older, and on my own, with no one but me to answer to.

God bless Mom and Dad, Troy, Jupiter – rest his soul – and the boys, Josh, Tim, and Rick. Thank you, God, for giving me those few hours of . . . BLISS.

More soon, L.

P.S. I am feeling like each time I think about tonight I change it a little bit. The boys get a little bit more rough with me each time. I get more seductive, and I make them tell me how they feel when they touch me. I make them tell me what it's like for them. I don't know why I changed it . . . I loved it the way it was, but when I make it again in my head, I make them do things a little nastier. I like that feeling. *I like that they feel more than I do.*

Last night, for the first time in ages, I slept all the way through the night. When I woke up, I couldn't even remember the dreams I had had, or if I even had any. I know they say everyone dreams all the time, but usually I remember them. Anyway, I was brushing Troy at the stables, and all of a sudden I got this image in my head of an address: 1400 River Road, 1400 River Road. I had dreamed it. I suddenly felt like I had to be there. I had to find this place and see what it was. I decided I would call Mom from the stables and tell her I was going for a ride with Troy, and I'd be back soon.

I had a little bit of an idea of where 1400 River Road was, but I just checked it with Zippy to make sure. He said it wasn't that far away, but there wasn't much there. I told him I wanted to ride out with Troy somewhere I hadn't been before. I didn't want to tell him I'd dreamed about this address and had to find out if it even existed. I was afraid he'd look at me funny, and besides, I wasn't even sure why I felt so drawn to it. I guess with all that had been happening, I felt like I should just keep quiet about it. Keep it secret, like so many other things. Zippy said to be sure to make a left when the dirt road forks off, because otherwise I would end up on a paved road, and that would be bad for Troy's hooves and shoes. I promised, and off we went.

All sorts of thoughts went through my head, and I even cried a little because I started to think about Josh and Tim and Rick, and how I would probably never see them again. I thought about how Donna hadn't called me today yet, and I was worried she was thinking

I was dirty or bad or something, and I felt a very deep need to talk to her. I hope she doesn't stop liking me.

I don't know what I would do if that happened. So, I kept seeing this address in my head, each time I finished a thought, no matter what it was, and finally I found myself in front of this very old, abandoned gas station. I got off Troy and tied him up at the frame that was still there. The frame that goes around the top of the pumps. The one with the signs telling you which gas is which. Grass was growing there, and I just let him graze so I could look around.

When I walked around Troy, so that I was completely facing the station, I saw the Log Lady standing very quiet with her log, right underneath the piece of wood that said 1400 River Road. She smiled at me, and I realized I had seen her face in my dream. We didn't say anything to each other for a long time. We just stared, smiling. I wasn't uncomfortable, but I was pretty curious about what I was there for, and just as I was thinking this, she spoke to me.

She said, 'I know you're feeling curious about this place and about me.'

I nodded.

'A dream told me I was supposed to meet you here, so that we could spend some time,' she said.

My stomach did a flip and my mouth dropped open.

'I dream like other people sometimes,' she said calmly. 'It just happens.'

I never realized that Margaret, the Log Lady, was so nice. We sat together on the grass out in the front, and she told me she knew a lot of things about me, special things. She said I should not worry so often. If I pay attention to the things around me, these special things will come.

She would often touch her log, be silent as she leaned down close to listen to it. Most times she would smile as if she were amused, pleased. Other times, she would tell the log that she would not hear about that now. This was not the time.

The last time that happened, she turned to me and whispered, '*Things are not what they seem.*'

. She looked away, then turned back with a different look on her face, as if she were relieved we were still alone. She said she knew I had been dreaming of being a woman, and that this was good because young girls always do. Then her words got confusing . . . she said many things about the woods, and I tried to listen very carefully, because I trusted her and thought maybe she knew something that would help me. A lot of it seemed like gibberish. I remember it, so I'll write it down, but I don't know what it means. Maybe I'll understand it later. What I did understand made me feel so good inside, like I wasn't being bad all of this time, maybe, and that I could keep on hoping for things without being afraid that I was acting selfishly.

Here are some of the things she told me. She said that sometimes the woods are a place to learn about things, and to learn about yourself. Other times the woods are a place for other creatures to be, and it is not for us. She said that sometimes people go camping and learn things they shouldn't. *Children are prey sometimes* . . . I think that's how she said it. What else . . .? I tried so hard to remember everything. Oh. She told me that she would be watching, and some day people will find out that she sees things and remembers them.

She said that it is important to remember things you see and feel. Owls are sometimes big. There! That was the one I had forgotten totally. *Owls are sometimes big*. I hope that doesn't mean my mom talked about that 'Owl Dream' I had. I don't think so, but that's the only way it makes any sense to me. I hope I'll understand all of this soon. Either way, we kept sitting together, and I listened to her hum this song that I had never heard before, but I thought it was very nice. It made me feel safe, which I think she was trying to make me feel. I feel sorry for her, that people think she is strange and weird. She isn't at all.

I could see in her eyes that something had hurt her, but I didn't even begin to understand what it was until Mom told me when I got home. She said that Margaret (the Log Lady) had a husband who was a fire fighter. He was killed fighting a fire, and Mom said it was awful because he tripped over a root or something and fell headfirst into hot coals and burned himself to death, face first. They had just been married a little while when he died, and since then Margaret has been very quiet and has kept her pain to herself. Mom also said that she didn't have her log until after her husband died.

I didn't know any of this when I was out there at 1400 River Road with her, but it didn't really matter, I guess. I told her I thought she was a very nice and special person, and that I was glad I had paid attention to my dream, because I wouldn't have wanted to miss talking with her. I told her I hoped she was right about my life having special things in it, that I will look for them, because I want my life to be good.

Then I told her something that I hope she never repeats. I didn't even expect to say it, and to tell you the truth I didn't know where it came from. I told her that sometimes things happen that no one knows about.

They happen in the woods when it is very dark. I told her that sometimes I wasn't even sure these things were real, and sometimes I think they are more real than the sun coming up in the morning, and that the thought of that frightened me very much. She looked away from me, I remember, when I finished. I thought I had said something that upset her. She grabbed her log tight, then looked back at me and said that I was a very beautiful girl, and that many people would love me in my life.

I hope many people do love me in my life. Some day someone will love me the way the boys did, but even more. I wonder where that person is right now, and if he is wondering where I am and what I look like, and when we will finally meet. I wonder if Margaret has ever thought about sex the way that I do.

On the way home I tried to hum the song she had hummed to me, but I couldn't remember it. I felt very good inside when I left 1400 River Road, and that feeling stayed with me, all through my ride back to the stables, all the way home with Mom in the car, and even now it is just as strong. I hope Margaret isn't feeling lonely right now. I hope she is feeling as happy as I am. I only wish I could have brought her news of how happy her life would be. It's too bad I had nothing for her.

More later, Laura

P.S. Donna still hasn't called me back.

LISTENING TO THE WOOD

Inside the trees are souls I think
Souls that grow and change
Inside each leaf, so quiet
A memory of moments no one else has seen
But no man ever listens
Takes the time to think
That trees might see what happens
That in the way they rustle
Is a hint they wish to speak.

They might have tried to whisper
In the palm of someone's hand
their memory of the little girl
How there is a new hole inside her
And a new and smaller mouth
But no one believes or cares
That maybe
The tree would know
Something was very wrong
That it wants to talk about the sadness
It has seen so many nights
I think the world
Should walk deep into the woods
Listen very carefully,
To the voices in the leaves.
See the details, the tiny maps
Of footsteps, and sometimes stains
They should see that the leaves
Are shaped like tears
They should study the design in fallen needles
Maybe there are some markings on the ground

That will lead the world
To the one who made
The hole.

It is late, and he came tonight. I don't know if the Log Lady was talking about the right Laura Palmer.

Dear Diary, November 20, 1985

I had a dream just now that makes me believe I will not be sleeping tonight.

I was in a room. It was very empty, and I was feeling badly that it was empty. I thought it was my fault that nothing was there. I was crouched in one of the corners of the room, and I was staring at this one spot at the other end of the room, because I knew something was going to be there, soon.

After a minute, I started to get very cold. And I thought that I saw something, but it disappeared. Then I looked away because I was trying to find the door that went to another room and out of this one, because I wanted to see if the furniture was in another room. I felt very bad about something and I wanted to fix things, so that I could stop feeling so . . . guilty. I guess that's what I was feeling. Guilt.

I turned back to look across the room and there was an enormous rat sitting there. I knew in the dream that it was coming after me, and that it wanted to bite my foot off. I became so afraid! I saw it come closer and closer to me and I tried to think of a way to stop it, or a place to run away, but there wasn't anywhere to go, or anything I could do!

I know it may sound funny, but it was so frightening. I sat very still and tried to keep my feet right against my body so that the rat couldn't get to my foot. I couldn't stop thinking of how awful it was going to feel when it closed its jaws around my ankle and bit down. I didn't want to feel that, and I didn't want the rat to come near me. Don't come near me! I just kept thinking of how much pain there would be . . . And so, in the dream, because I knew all he wanted was my foot, *I bit my foot off myself*.

When I woke up, I could barely breathe, I was so scared! I can still see the rat, and I think it was after me because something was wrong with the room, or I was being punished for something. But I was more afraid of the rat's teeth and how much it would hurt . . . So I decided I would do it. I would hurt myself, before he could. Even though I didn't understand why the rat wanted to hurt me, I just knew I had to do it myself, or he would.

I didn't like that dream at all. Please, Diary, I know it sounds silly, but don't judge me the way someone might if they heard me tell them this dream. I hope I never dream like that again. I don't even want to know what it means, or if I'm sure I even want to remember it. I'll decide that tomorrow, when the darkness is gone, and things are easier to see when they come after you.

It makes me mad that I feel like I can't go and tell Mom about this. I'm afraid she'll laugh and then maybe tell it to everyone and embarrass me. I'm so afraid people will laugh at me. I am going to try to be more like Donna. I'll be good and I'll do everything I'm supposed to do. That way, there won't be anything anyone can find out and make fun of me for. There will be nothing they can say I have done wrong.

I bet that what I did with Donna and the boys is causing this. I can't even think straight enough to decide if one feeling was worth the other. Something has to be causing nights like this. I will try to be better. I will stop doing things that older girls should be doing. I will not let anyone hurt me, like in the dream. *I'll hurt myself first.* I know the places that are the most delicate. I'll do the hurting from now on, as long as all of this stops!!!!

I wish I could talk to my mommy.

Laura

Dear Diary,   December 16, 1985

I don't know that I will be writing in you for a
while. I have just had another dream. I must have
fallen asleep while I was waiting for the sun.

I don't know why, but I kept seeing you appear and
disappear on people's laps. On their seats at the diner,
when they went to the jukebox. On the hood of their
cars when they went to go driving. I tried to take you
back, but you kept sliding away. You were going to
tell everyone what was inside you.

A few people read what was written there and these
people turned into rats. They wanted to take me out
the way BOB does. I think that until I understand
more, we shouldn't speak. I don't know why I dreamed
this . . . but I am too afraid to challenge it.

If this doesn't make the nightmares and the fire and
the ropes and the little silver blades go away . . .
Maybe I am supposed to give into them. Maybe that is
what is meant for me. Maybe I just have to be patient
and stop fighting it, and it will go away.

I hate to say goodbye to a listener as good as you. I
feel I must, though, until I find out if you are somehow
talking to people when I don't know about it.

Am I going crazy? I can't wait until vacation is over
and school starts again so that I can have something to
keep me busy. I look at other girls that I know, other
girls I see, and they all smile, like I do. Inside are they
beginning to lose everything they know? Have they
stopped trusting themselves and everyone around them
too? Please don't let me find out that I am the only
one on earth with this pain.

                                            Laura

Dear Diary,   April 23, 1986

It has been a long time since I've written. School is
fine but I find it almost too easy. There is not enough
to keep my mind from wandering to boys, or fantasies.
Donna and I have had several fights this year because
she says I'm acting strangely to her, and that I'm not
being the friend that I was. I hate crying, so why does
it come so easily lately? I am only trying to be good,
and to keep busy, and not to do too much talking or
daydreaming because I thought that bothered people
and made bad things happen to me.

Now Donna is mad because I won't tell her what
I'm really feeling, because I'm afraid! I can't tell her
I'm afraid because she would make me tell her why. I
can never ever tell. I haven't even touched myself
where I know I can to make myself feel good. I'm
afraid, because that is about sex, and I decided I
wouldn't think about that any more ... which is so
hard!!!

I hate myself, and I hate my life! Dad has been busy
all the time lately with Benjamin and his work there at
the Great Northern, and I am starting to feel the way
Audrey must when her father spends more time and
attention with me than he does with her. Now it is
happening in the reverse, and I am just trying to be
good and make it stop, and it is only getting harder for
me to sleep or even eat! I don't want to feel this way
any more. If I do, I know something awful will
happen.

I dreamed last night that I had dug a hole in the
backyard for a well, because I was trying to help us
with water, and I thought a well would be a nice thing
to build for the family. Mom loved the idea and

smiled very big. But when she went outside, later in the dream, I was burying myself in the hole, trying to kill myself. She realized I had lied to her, and this made her very upset. She ran out to stop me, and I screamed that I didn't want to wake up in the middle of the night with leaves all over me any more. I wanted to be a tree so that I could listen for trouble in the woods. And I was buried all of a sudden. But I was inside something that wasn't a dirt hole.

Mom came to my room right after to ask if I was all right, and I told her I was fine. I was just having nightmares about the woods is all. The look on her face went from sadness to hopefulness. Then, unfortunately, she began something I didn't need to hear at all! She started telling me about the birds and the bees, and about birth control and babies, and all of this ridiculous stuff about how my dreams were just a part of my changing body, and maybe I just needed some questions answered.

The whole time she talked to me, I was thinking of something else.

I had to think of flowers and of smiling faces and anything . . . big trucks filled with lumber, of birds, of Donna Donna Donna . . . good things only. Don't listen, couldn't listen to that voice saying all of the things that were like little keys to the doors and rooms I wasn't supposed to be in! How could this happen? She didn't stop for almost an hour, and I almost had to hold my hand down . . . I wanted to hit her, smack that smiling, helpful face and scream, 'How do you do it! What has happened to that part of me!'

Do you want to know the part that frightens me most? The only thing people think about me right now is that I am going through my adolescence! Everyone still sees the smiling Laura Palmer. The girl with perfect grades and perfect hair and perfect little fingers that want to sometimes, late at night, go into the mirror to strangle the daydreaming troublemaker I see in the reflection!

Today I will go to see Donna and I'll talk to her. I'll talk the best I can. I have no schoolwork left to do, and I've already finished two extra-credit projects. I made the honor roll, and the junior debate team. I pray all of the time, but have never felt worse in my life. I am starting to think that a few moments of good, in the middle of miles and ages of bad, is better than no good at all. I hope Donna still wants to be my friend.

If I can, I will tell you what happens with Donna.

Soon, Laura

A memory of skipping
I was small, looking up at him
Before he told me to lie down
Or to say things
Before he told me
That opening my mouth was bad
That we had a secret
Before he began to turn me inside out
With his dirty claws
Before I sat on the tiny hill
We used to skip
Hold hands
Talk about what we saw
He told me what to see
But I didn't see it
I have been blind
I think
Ever since the skipping stopped.

I want to be left alone like other people are. I want to learn about this soft white suit I wear the way everyone else does.

I want to forget the things that suddenly come to me . . . Something very bad is happening . . . Why is it happening to me?

I think it is real. I think it is real!

After I see Donna, maybe I can tell you about what I am remembering. I had forgotten so much . . . but I can't tell if I am better off knowing or not really knowing at all.

Please still be my friend, Donna, please!

L

I spent the day with Donna yesterday. For a long time she wouldn't even really say anything to me. When I started crying, I ran out of her house and just kept running. I was so glad when she came after me, and she was crying too. I told her as much as I could. That I was worried about being good because I had been having bad dreams, very bad dreams, and I wasn't just kidding her when I said I wasn't sleeping at all. I told her I wished we could talk about the night with the guys at the stream, but it always seems like she hates me or something, or I'll have an awful dream and think that what happened was bad. I told her I needed to hear what she thought about that night. I needed to know if she thinks we should be punished for it, or if I should, because I did more than she did . . . I just needed to know!

Donna told me that she was afraid I wasn't talking to her because I was mad that she hadn't gone as far with the guys as I had, and that I didn't like her any more because of it! I asked her how she could think that when we had such a nice hug when the evening was over, and I still remember that hug as one of the clearest, nicest parts of the whole night! I told her I was just very confused, and I told her I didn't know half the time whether I should be enjoying it as much as I was, or if I should have been feeling bad.

Donna said the only reason she got out of the water was that she wasn't sure what she felt right doing, even though all of the boys were nice. And then she cried and looked at me, very strange, and said something that really made me feel weird. She said that another reason she didn't get more into it was that she was afraid to because I seemed too good at it right away, and she didn't know what she should be doing, or how to do it. She wanted to know if it just came naturally to me, or if I had been seeing a boy and hadn't told her.

I couldn't answer her for a long time. I don't think I knew the answer. What did she mean, good at it? I told her I remembered feeling sexy, and very happy that they liked me and wanted me, but half of that, if not more, was the boys' doing, not mine.

Plus we were drunk that night, and it just felt so good to do things I had wondered about for so long ... She stopped me there and said that she thought about boys like that too. I asked her how she thought of them, like what they were doing when she dreamed of them, and she said they were taking her dancing, or seeing her at school and letting her ride in their cars. She said she was thinking about being with older boys who treated her like she was a princess, and at night they would come into this big, beautiful bed and lie next to her, and they would talk and kiss, and sometimes they would make love.

She said she didn't really like going that far because it seemed too rough for the rest of the daydream. She thinks about sex, though, she said. But it is the kind of sex that goes really slow like in soap operas. She said she sees it in slow motion and she can hear music playing, and they roll around, she and this boy, very slow, until it fades out of her head. She said she hoped that my fantasies were as sexy as hers are.

Oh, God, Diary, everything was fine until we talked about that! I just had to tell her that my fantasies were exactly the same as hers, and that we should never have argued, and I said I was sorry if I hurt her feelings. I should have been more open with her, and that I was only worried that she had begun to hate me for going so far that night. She said she thought I was very brave, and that if it felt good to me, then I should think of it as a good thing. *But what about the fantasies she has!* I was about to die when I heard how pure and sweet and gentle they were. Why doesn't she think the things I do! I was so hoping we had the same thoughts . . . I was depending on it.

I know she was telling the truth because of how she told me, and by how embarrassed she got when she talked about this boy getting into bed with her. She is so pure, I just can't believe it. I think that the times that I have to go into the woods at night have poisoned me.

I would be like Donna, I'll bet, if I were still just skipping through the trees, instead of . . . what happens now. But . . . I would never ever ever wish for what happens now! I wish for things that make me feel sexy and playful, things that don't take me to do all the work, things like someone else trying to please me, instead of me always trying to make everyone else happy.

I wish there was a place you could go where someone would answer all of your questions, and tell you if you were doing the right thing or not. How am I supposed to know when I can't even talk about things really? I just keep saying the same things again and again. I am running in circles, and it is time that I stop.

Donna and I are friends still, and I still love her, but things feel different to me. I can't think the way she does, or even try to any more. I will think what I feel, and I will try to make people see things the way I do. I wish I had a marijuana cigarette right now. It feels like I haven't laughed for years and years and years.

Thank you for listening.

Laura

I am just going to write and not think too hard about it and maybe I can remember more. I just woke up; it is 4:12 a.m.

I don't remember when it started, but he has always had long hair. He knows everything about me and knows how to frighten me more than any of the dreams I have already told you about.

He first started to play with me. We would chase each other through the woods, and he would always find me . . . but I could never find him. He would come up from behind me and grab my shoulders and ask me my name. I would tell him it was Laura Palmer, and he would let go and turn me around and laugh.

When I think about it, he wasn't playing the way he should have been. He was being very mean to me, and he was scaring me all the time. I think he likes it when I am frightened. He makes me feel that way every time he takes me with him. He likes to embarrass me by pulling down my panties and putting his fingers inside, deep. When he knows it hurts me, he pulls them out and smells his hand. He always tells me I smell like bad things. He screams out loud into the trees that I smell, and that I am dirty, and he doesn't know why he even likes me. He says if I didn't beg him to come all of the time, he would never come back.

I never beg him to come. Never. I wish him far away from here. I swear it.

When I started to get older, he would tell me things about myself that I didn't know. I don't think he was telling the truth. I think he was lying to me and making it up as he went along. He always knew exactly what scared me, and just the things to say to make me cry. Then he would take my neck . . . and squeeze. He squeezed my neck hard until I stopped crying. He would let go just before I would faint . . . I think I was fainting . . . sometimes that still happens. Everything goes tingly and dark, and my head spins inside and I can't see anything, and I have to stop crying or he'll keep squeezing.

Sometimes he says, 'What's this down here? . . . What's this down here, Laura Palmer?' He always says my whole name like he won't get close to me like that, but he will every other way. Sometimes I would come home bleeding. I would bleed and I couldn't tell anyone, so I would sit up all night in my bathroom, all alone, and wait for it to stop coming out. Sometimes he would cut me between my legs, and other times he would cut me inside my mouth. Always tiny little cuts, hundreds of tiny little cuts. I had to use a flashlight in the bathroom or else my parents might wake up and see the light, and I'd be in worse trouble then.

Some nights he would make me sticky. Rub himself very fast, and he would say that I had to hold the sticky in my hands, close my eyes, and recite this little poem while I licked my hands clean.

I only remember a little. This hasn't happened for a long time, the sticky. He made me say:

> The little bitch
> Is awfully sorry
> The little bitch
> Drinks you up

(I can't remember more, except the last line.)

In this seed is death indeed.

He wants me to like it, when he is with me. He wants me to say that I am dirty and that I have an odor. I should be thrown into the river so that I will be clean.

I am so careful to smell clean, all the time. I always wash between my legs, and I always go to sleep in fresh panties, in case he makes me come with him. I always worry he will come for me, and I won't have clean panties. He says I'm lucky he even stays to spend time around me. He says that he is the only man who will ever want to touch me.

He comes to the window, and I see him. I always see him, and he is always smiling like we are going to have a good time together. I am so close to calling my parents for help, but I am afraid of what would happen. I can't let anyone know about him. If I keep seeing him, he might get tired of me and go away. Maybe if I stopped fighting him, he would not like to visit me any more. If I weren't afraid. If I could just not feel afraid . . .

I have never thought about him like this ever before.

I hope that if there is a God, he will understand that I am trying to keep clean, and if this is a test that he is giving me, I'll find a way to pass it. I bet it is a test. I bet God wants me to prove that I can take orders, or maybe that I am not afraid to die and come be with him. Maybe BOB knows God, and that is why he always knows what I am feeling inside. God must be telling him what to do to me. God wants me not to be afraid, maybe, of being dirty. If I'm not afraid, he'll take me to heaven.

I hope so.

L

I have been trying very hard not to be afraid.

I am seeing a boy I told you about once before. I didn't like him then, but now I think he is just right for me. He reminds me very much of the boy on the wall of the Book House. He dresses the same way, but he does not have a motorcycle. I am fourteen now. I didn't let anyone celebrate my birthday. I made Mom promise she wouldn't plan anything. I told her at the kitchen table the day before that I had a lot of thinking to do about my life. I just wanted to spend my birthday alone. I wanted to walk alone, and maybe take Troy out for a ride: I made sure she knew I didn't want to hurt her feelings, but I just needed to spend some time alone. She fussed for a while and kept asking me why I couldn't spend the following day by myself. I finally told her that I was feeling confused and I wanted to come home on the night of my birthday with everything sorted out. I wasn't going to go far, I promised her that. I just wanted to go. I promised her that next year and the following year, sweet sixteen, I will have a party of one kind or another.

So I spent my birthday alone. I went out to where I go with BOB. It was light out, and everything seemed like an awful dream, until I saw a piece of rope lying at the back of the base of his favorite tree. I got a chill, but forced it away. I tried to look carefully at the tree, to find something that would explain why he picked this place, this tree. There was nothing. I made sure I was alone before I did what I had planned.

I looked very carefully, and when I knew I was alone, I pulled a marijuana cigarette from my pocket. I made Bobby get one for me. He wanted to share but I told him he couldn't. We could do some together later, maybe. I smoked it very slowly and started thinking about sex. About men, all kinds of them, inside me.

I tried to think of things that BOB would like. I pulled a pair of my panties out of my pocket and rubbed them on the tree. I wore them just before I left to come here, so I knew the smell of me would be strong . . . I'm not afraid any more either that I smell bad. I know I don't. I think I smell like a girl should.

When I put my panties to my own nose and breathe in, I imagine a girl in front of me, and how a man would want to touch her. Get up close. BOB calls it pussy. I want to touch, can you hear me, BOB! When I smell it, I am not afraid, I told myself. I said it out loud many times while I was there, smoking and thinking of all sorts of ways I could touch Bobby . . . Things I would like to make him do. I thought every thought I could that would call BOB to come. I think he was there, but he was hiding.

So I got very stoned, all by myself, and pushed myself on to the dirt, sliding on to the leaves and pine needles on the ground, and I looked up into the great tree. I wanted the tree to watch me, memorize the face of the new little girl who came to lie down. The old one is gone. She had to go off. I only use her voice sometimes; it is so much easier to get what I want when I say it sweetly, and like a little girl. I took off my clothes and began to touch my breasts, lick my fingers, and then rub my nipples with the wetness. I made circles the way the boys do with their tongues. I made noises when it felt good. I cried out when I pinched them hard and made them pink.

The wind began to come up, and I felt it move over my bare chest, and I remember saying, 'Ohh, whoever that is, I like that ... Yes ... I like that very much ...' I felt myself get a little wet inside my panties ... so I undressed completely and I talked to BOB out loud, while I touched my secret button. I said, 'BOB ... Bobby ... Laura has a sweet muffin here for you ... Nice and clean and ... mmmmmmm ... I'll bet it tastes good too ... Come out, BOB ... come out and play ...' The wind picked up, but I never saw BOB.

I came like I never have before. My body just couldn't stop, and I had to grab on to the tree, peel off bark in one place, grab again, dig in with my nails ... and then it slowed. I was so warm with the marijuana and my little show for the woods that I almost took a nap, there, lying naked. But I couldn't do that. I won this one. He hadn't shown up. Night or day doesn't count. I showed him I wasn't afraid. I touched myself under his tree. I called to him and made him the fool. I'm going to pass this test ... you'll see. If BOB wants nasty, all I need is a little time. *I can be the bad girl he wants.*

On the way out of the woods, I was nearly killed as an owl swooped down out of nowhere. I could feel the power in his wings as he shot by me. I thought of the Log Lady. Something she has said:

'Many things are not what they seem.'

This used to seem frightening to me. This place, the slightest thought of touching myself, and teasing myself, frightened me. No more. No, this place I visited is not what it seemed. I see now that it is a place of darkness, but I love it. *I welcome it.* I will not fight it, even when it slips deep inside and cuts me. I have found light and pleasure inside this horror. I am not done with my plan.

I'll be back, BOB. I'll be back to open and close around you like you thought I never would. I'll be back.

Laura

Just to fill you in, I did spend the rest of the day
with Troy at the stables. Being around him relaxed
me, and I went home later that evening feeling very
strong, very new inside. I did not entertain any
thoughts of being bad, or wrong, by doing this. I was
going to stop being hurt and taunted by this man. A
man I know only by his first name. I do not know
where he lives, or where he comes from. But I will get
him back. There's no fun in a game of torture if the
victim is screaming for more.

That was almost two weeks ago ... no, maybe a
week. I am very deep in concentration lately. Seeing
Bobby Briggs is fun. He is anywhere I want him to be,
with anything I want him to bring. Just yesterday, I
decided he had waited too long to be with me the way
he wanted. I, too, was tired of the process of petting
and going home feeling like a cork had been stuck
inside me, that it had trapped everything I so wished
to let go. But I had to let him think I was the fourteen-
year-old I appear to be ...

Mom and Dad left for the entire afternoon, and I
told them I'd be out for almost as long as they would
be, but that I wanted to help with supper that night,
so I would be home no later than six-thirty. Mom's
face shined at the sound of such words. I have to keep
my parents happy. I have to keep loving them, like
their little girl should. I have to support what I have
not chosen, but have, quite simply, been given. Two
lives. *Two very different lives.*

The naughtier Laura had a date with Bobby Briggs
in Low Town. He said he knew of an abandoned barn
out where no one would find us. I liked the idea that I

would have him alone some place where I could go kinda crazy on him. I was nervous, for a bit, because I suddenly realized that this was not the BOB I hated, but the young Bobby who swaggered up to smiling Laura Palmer and asked if she would be his. No matter, I'd play him like he needed me to. I knew he was aware that I had never made love with a boy before . . . I knew it would be different with someone who took care . . . I knew it might pull me back to thirteen years old, when I learned to love a man's hands in a stream late at night and cried because he was gone so soon afterward. I couldn't let that come up. I knew I had to be strong. I could have BOB watching me right now . . . at any moment. I couldn't fall in love . . . certainly not out loud.

Bobby was charming and I could tell he was nervous because he couldn't get his words out very well, and the blanket he brought on the back of his bike wasn't opening as he tried, diligently, to spread it.

This made him very nervous, because I was balancing a bottle of vodka, a small one for two, and a marijuana cigarette (some smoke) in between my fingers, and I didn't have as good a grasp as I would have liked, and I had to fall to my knees to avoid breaking anything.

He felt very bad, but I turned it around so that he had been more of a hero than a dunce. He was neither, but I allowed him to lift me to my feet and steady me with his arms. I could think only of how I just wanted to take a drink and do some smoke so I could relax. Things come much easier for me when I am loose, and feeling confident. One of the reasons I most enjoy Bobby is that he can get me smoke any time I want . . . he can have a friend buy us alcohol, any time I want. I like the way that feels, that kind of devotion. I enjoy the way he moves, little tiny waves inside him, when I lean in close and say, 'I can't wait, but let's take our time.' His immediate smile and his readiness to let me take over first.

I, after all, was for the first time beginning a sexual experience with interest, and affection. A little control of my own. I knew he would take over, once he felt I'd let him. But for now, if he was to keep bringing me little treats all the time, I wanted him to feel it was worth it . . . that he hadn't chosen a dead fish, like I promised I would never be.

An hour later, after taking my time with his lips, and occasionally feeding him the smoke, or vodka, I was ready, and I told him to lie back and imagine whatever he wished. I told him to build a dream inside his head, and to let his imagination follow me. It was just for him, we both knew that. I put him, hard, into my mouth, and had a picture in my head of BOB's hand as he did himself . . . as he put my hand on it . . . and then I was back in the barn. I slowed it down, found the rhythm he liked, and I kept my tongue moving inside and I went up and down him, following the noises he made, the whines . . . listening with delicacy, making sure I kept him where he wanted to be. This time was not about teasing him in and out of his pleasure. He came the way I dream men do . . . with suddenness after a long internal climb, sitting upright with a look of amazement and awe . . . gratification. A smile.

We spent another hour or so buried in each other, until it had to happen and he slipped inside. I opened my eyes and saw him as his eyes fell closed. I forced the memory of wanting this . . . away. Feeling like that would be so easy, and yet, I could not become weak.

We moved together, and I found it easier to handle, easier to really enjoy, with my eyes closed. I could move with him, roll around to the top, place his hands where I love to feel them. He is so good to me, without any words. I wanted him to know how wonderful it felt, locked there inside, never wanting to leave, just wanting more and more of me! We rolled and pushed and pulled at each other and came apart hours later, when it was impossible that we do more.

I felt truly satisfied, like years of taunting and emotional pulling and pushing had been set free. The steel bar I imagined holding me upright was *flexing*, turning to flesh, and melting. The tension and the anxiousness I felt for so long, about how it would be when someone really wanted me. Not because they wanted me to weep or to die slowly of a sadness I could not name. Someone who cared how it felt to me, wanted to make sure it was nice. I felt like I should feel, like all girls should feel . . . but I could not forget that there were other worlds to think of. Other moments. Rude awakenings at the darkest hours of night. A man in my window, smiling . . . offering a challenge by waving a black glove. I lay there wondering if he would come soon, or if by my simply deciding he no longer frightened me, he was somehow eliminated.

I couldn't rely on dreams like that. And suddenly, there was a terrible problem. A terrible and sad problem that I had to face without the emotion I so wanted to give! From Bobby's mouth came, slowly, small words of love, then confessions. Soon after, promises of loyalty and happiness for ever.

Laura, Laura, I can't let you hear this. Just watch his lips move, do not listen, I told myself, over and over. But Bobby meant it. He was, after all, the boy who had admired me for years, who had tugged on my ponytails for as long as I wore them, and soon after made a point to pass me at least once a day in the hallways at school, or to catch my eye in class. Smile, as if it were an unexpected sight.

I knew he had planned this. But the Laura who loved him back, the young girl who so desperately hoped he would come after her, when the time was right, cannot come out to play. She is inside resting. Deep inside, cradled in the braver half. The one that finds this Bobby boy satisfying, yes, but not interesting beyond that. There is no strength in him . . . no challenge. I'll keep him with me, save him for her, when it is safe for her to come back. But these words of love are too real, too innocent. This boy, so young, is merely a messenger to the Laura that is living here now.

I was forced to do something cruel. Something that would make him, perhaps, rethink the entire idea of Laura. He had to see her as something he never thought existed. I had to laugh at him. Hard. Laugh until his eyes lost their light. I had to shoot him down, couldn't let him be so appealing to the same young Laura that BOB wants. The one I'm sure he's waiting for. To save myself, I had to laugh in the face of a boy, who now may never be so honest again.

I had to do it! Why does it hurt so badly to protect myself? Where was this love when I was on my knees begging for it? Dammit. I know I hurt him . . . I hope some day he will understand why. I would never crush someone the way I was crushed. Had I been the one laughed at, I don't know that I would ever stand as straight again – never approach someone with even the smallest compliment, because the memory of laughter would still ring in my ears.

I am ashamed and confused again by the things that happen to me. Is this a trick that BOB is playing on me? Another test? Ruining my chance at love with the right boy, by forcing me to humiliate him, the way I have been and have now turned cold and bitter because of its scars? ... Will Bobby pick himself up and see that I did not mean it? Or have I been tricked into spoiling a romance I could have been protected by at least during the day?

What does life want from me? What have I done, and what do I do now?! I only wanted to stop the pain, not to begin spreading it myself.

I'm thinking ... I'm thinking.

Everything that had to be done has been done. If this is something BOB did, then it will only cause him an amazing victory if I show any regret ... any ... *remorse*. I cannot care. I must believe Bobby will come back, tail wagging. If he does not, I shall master the whistle he responds to. Let the boy earn my attention outside the barn lust, outside the kisses I give out only when I feel like it, never just because. I'll become a professional at not feeling anything.

I'll find a way to do it. I can't give up. I don't even believe half the time that what I'm living is real. I am lost. Lost. But a stronger, more manipulating Laura is rearing her head, and opening herself to threats and games played only in the dark.

When I find out who he is, I'll make him known to everyone!

To a New Strength, Laura

Dear Diary,   August 3, 1986

It is a little after ten p.m. on the evening of the
disaster with Bobby Briggs. I am surprised to say that
he phoned not fifteen minutes ago, and . . . somehow,
in a mass of words that were sounding more rehearsed
than heartfelt, he apologized for being too quick to
recite such oaths of love when maybe I didn't find that
attractive in a boy. That maybe I wanted someone
who had to be broken a bit, before it all came out . . .
He told me he meant what he had said, but was wrong
to say it so quickly.

The whole thing sounded like it had been picked
word for word out of the dictionary or thesaurus,
and I couldn't help but wish for a moment that I
was dead. Here he is apologizing for something I,
and I'm certain girls everywhere, even outside of the
Peaks, dream of hearing a boy say. He's chosen his
words carefully, tried to prove he is still, hours after
his orgasm, in love. Another miracle . . . and what
do I do? I am forced to keep silent on the phone, to
stifle words of love, from my own heart, simply out
of the fear that this is all part of a grand scheme to
drive me, no brakes in the fast lane, down the road
of insanity.

I am trapped inside a part of me I hate. A hard,
masculine part of myself that has surfaced to fight,
after small memories and scars come out of me with
a suddenness that is sobering as well as horrifying –
and I fight to save the Laura I wish I could be
again. The one everyone thinks is still around. Me
in a sundress, hair in the wind, and a smile engraved

into my cheeks by the sharp fear that a man may
visit me at any moment this evening and try to kill
me.

L

Dear Diary,   August 4, 1986
                                         3:30 a.m.

It comes to me now that I have decided to play
along. After repeating it to myself for ages it seems, I
finally feel a sense of resolve with my joining him for
the sole purpose of battle. To join the darkness, and
perhaps cling to the bit of light remaining inside me,
and use it as the strength it should always have been.

Ah, the fairness of life. That special moment when a
hand flies up whether visible or verbal, screaming,
STOP, she is dying! This child is dying without a
safety feature everyone else seems to wrestle with, as if
it were an inconvenience.

I searched carefully and have found a space inside
me that says that it is almost too late, mine are not the
eyes of a girl of fifteen, but the eyes of someone who
has been afraid to look around herself and to question
the simplest of things. My mind, it continues, is not
the mind of a young girl who imagines life to be a
series of warm sweaters, while the cold spell passes by.

It warns me that the mind in which I live belongs to
someone who knows too much of life and how it ends
most often without warning. How it deals us blows,
dares us to dream when in fact there is no use. Manages
to leave out that there is a plan etched in the planet for
me. This mind knows.

The reality that there is no choosing a day's events, or
even a moment's when before you've even opened your
eyes to see light for the very first time, someone of a
great evil and stealth chooses you. Spins a bottle of sorts
and giggles at the power in a simple game of selection.

                                         Laura

Dear Diary,   August 6, 1986
                               4:47 a.m.

I cannot let myself sleep because I have to see BOB
when he comes through the window. I have to be
ready.

I have thought a great deal about my life. I am aging
without my own permission. I believe when he comes
to take me, I will either leave home and return harmed
although satisfied by the brutal death of an enemy, or
I will never return. And in death admit silently I knew
not of my visitor's strength nor of his will.

For now I am half-numb, half-raw. A girl who still
manages to rise each morning and exit the place I lately
must be reminded is called home. As if nothing were less
noticeable than the trail of blood left behind me as I go.

I do not doubt that BOB is aware of my every
movement. That this horror who calls himself a man
sits up high when the sun shines or perhaps curls up
below. No matter. He watches me with eyes that
burrow inside, seeing each speck of doubt, sensing
each palpitation of my heart when a boy passes, each
embrace from a mother who knows nothing of how far
away her daughter's bedroom has become.

I try each day to memorize the face that looks back
at me in the mirror. I hold tight to it. I imagine I'll be
in flight when I compare it to my remains that I often
dream soon will be found.

I have such an anger and an urge to charge at the
sky, to call the wind a liar for never showing itself. An
urge to scream at the two who allowed my birth. Cries
for help to anyone who will hear them. To scream into
the street that there is a lack of miracles in Mother
Nature herself. *Her divinity is a lie.*

In a forest of trees again and again, I have been brought down. Surgery of a strange and indescribable nature takes place. Blood is let. This Mother Nature has not done away with this evil, nor has it opened its wood to allow a scream to escape. Instead, it cradles this man and keeps him safe from discovery, safe from daylight. He knows the planet will not betray him. This light will come, and stay, leave only to return on schedule. He has a promise. The universe's habit, conveniently requiring a twelve-hour fix of the two extremes.

His time is the evening, the hour during which rescue is least possible, and when most with pure hopes and dreams and memories of swinging on swing seats are fast asleep. Their eyes moving quickly under their lids. *Seeing nothing.*

Never is there a noise that stirs even those who sleep in the next room. Never does the world lean a bit for me, cast a vote, and cause an eye to open . . . See the man . . . see the way his eyes are frozen in the image of my face in a scream. No explanation for WHY he has chosen me, or even if he has a final plan.

I can only wait. Hold my tired eyes open with the energy of a dare. A fight to see who in fact is the darkest. Who, when forced to see the other side, will in fact survive?

I sit awaiting his arrival, kept awake by the notion that I shall grow accustomed to the dark far easier than he to the light.

Laura

Dear Diary, September 10, 1986

Enclosed please find my mind and its memory. As well, a characteristic the enemy lacks in excess – conscience. 'Guilt' is simply a word he uses to silence me. He has no regard for mortality, no concern for danger.

How could such an intruder fear death, or the possibility of imprisonment, and still manage to come so consistently up the side of my home, using my window as if it were familiar to him?

He mocks me, entering dressed in the clothes of one who could be a best friend. A neighbor. A traveling salesman who casually invites himself in, goes as far as to request coffee, regular, before dissolving into the daydream he sometimes is.

Does he expect to sit down and chat before taking the house's only child from her room and treating her like an experiment?

I am either dreaming him to life and slowly killing myself, or he has told my parents of his visits and has offered, in return for their own safety, that these visits will continue without possibility of interruption. They would simply go unnoticed. Junk mail, somewhere in the house. I imagine that they would have to hear me as I am led out. Is it possible they do not care?

L

Dear Diary,   September 11, 1986
                                     2:20 a.m.

I cannot tell you how much it upsets me that I am
no threat to him.

He is too safe with the idea that he will always gain
entrance to my home and exit painlessly and without
sound. In the dark he knows he will find a grip around
my wrist strong enough to silence me, and to carry
me, like a child drags a doll, to a place where he knows
no one will find me. He knows this because the place
is miles from any source of light other than that which
pours sometimes, so clearly in my memory, from his
lips and eyes – the very light stolen from within me.
The girl who, ever since she can remember, made a
patient effort to tolerate, and keep secret the very man
who wishes to steal her innocence, never allowing her
to mature, never permitting the joys of maturity. The
time this little girl has dreamed of ever since she knew
how to skip, and run, and smile at even the slightest
breeze, the way it tickled her so. Unselfishly, she gave
and gave of herself, emptying the delicate basket inside
her, of her soul.

I hope to call him to my window soon. I fear he is
waiting for me to tire of these all-night writing sessions. These moments where I lapse in and out of the
part of me who plans to open the window this time
and give my hand willingly. The part of me that
doubts anything really exists at all and that therefore
there is nothing at all to fear outside that window, and
so am willing to venture to the usual spot, without
struggle. I who swears a noise or powerful slap at the
back of the head will not cause even the slightest
change in footsteps. The part of me that has rehearsed

its cries for more and more incisions, more insertions, more insults and threats, and has planned to continue them until his appetite, before insatiable, grows smaller. The animal frozen solid in front of his shot-gun barrel, begging to fill that space on his wall.

Remove the thrill. Program yourself. There will be pain, but none worse than before. Hold tight on the image of home and of bed and of the warm smell of him as you rinse and rinse and rinse. Home awaits you as it always has.

Play with him as he plays with you. Accept that you are bad and dirty and cheap and should be thrown to the wolves as scrap meat, and must never bear children, for who knows the faces they would be locked behind from birth until death . . . Remember to ignore. Leave an opening large enough inside to take on his body weight in hatred and methods of reduction that only apply to the emotional portions of oneself, the most vital and irreplaceable of all.

Believe that he is only intrigued by the fear he breeds, the lack of interest you display in life when he leaves you back at your home. How he pretends to ring the doorbell, mocks you, your life, your hopes, your most private insecurities, watches as you struggle with the sense that you are unworthy to even enter the house in which you took your first steps, feel as he watches you catch a tear before it has left your eye – *look for him and he is gone.*

As if it were a religion, I have chanted inspirations to myself, for days now I have whined, and taunted, and almost wished him to arrive, and he has not. I have an incredible headache from trying to think of his weaknesses, when in fact, I couldn't begin to know them. Perhaps I am wrong altogether about his lust only for the fear in his particular victim . . . I must say honestly, I am tired of making light of the situation and believe that if I do not sleep soon, I shall begin seeing BOB everywhere. This, need I mention, would not be good for me at present.

I am lonely here, and find myself thinking about Bobby, who I know would hold me in his arms the way I can't imagine anyone else doing.

Be careful, Laura

Dear Diary,   October 1, 1986

I'm sorry I haven't written, but so much has
happened. Tonight as I began to undress for bed
Bobby Briggs came to my window. A beautiful,
dreamy sight that sent me reeling. He says there is a
party we couldn't miss out at the end of Sparkwood. A
friend of his, Leo – who I think I've heard of before in
the air of gossip that I often hunt down – is throwing a
party. I warned him, I had only thought seriously of
curling up with him, and confessed that I was missing
more sleep than I need to be sociable.

He promised me there would be no problem in the
alertness department, as he had a new treat for me to
try that sometimes negates the need for sleep entirely.

I'm out the window, Diary. Shhhh!

I'll tell all the moment I return. I'm hiding you . . .
beware of BOB . . . he is sometimes tardy.

                                        Laura

P.S. It just struck me that BOB's name is a warning
in itself . . .

    B. BEWARE
    O. OF
    B. BOB

Dear Diary,   October 3, 1986

I don't know where to begin! I returned home the
following afternoon, without a single gripe from the
watchdogs, Mom and Dad. I was halfway down the
side of the house when I realized I was heading way
out of upper town to a party filled with people at least
six to ten years my senior . . . and I was thinking I'd
be back by sunrise? Never! Not to mention that Bobby
had some 'Go Fast' for me somewhere . . . at least I
thought that to be the situation before we arrived at
Leo's . . . I'm guilty of the understatement of the year
with that one.

But anyway, I must first brag about the tangled web
I did weave, and how not a stitch was out of place or
questioned when I arrived back home at nearly six
p.m. the following day! Need I say, I have now crossed
over into a dimension of intense sleep deprivation?
Three days and four nights . . . and taking into consider-
ation the treat I was given as a door prize before
leaving, I could be up until next month, painlessly
dropping pound after pound . . . (six and a half since
the last day I slept). I find that no matter what drug, if
any, I have inside me, the less I sleep, the less I eat.

The note said something simple and to the point.
Skip it if it bores you, but I guess I gained a sense of
satisfaction and joy out of pulling the wool over the
'folks'' (as Bobby says) eyes.

*Mom, it is just about five a.m. and I have tried
again and again to get back to sleep. After almost
two solid hours of fair tries, I was suddenly
reminded of the clearing I spent the other afternoon
in. Troy so enjoyed the grazing there, and I think*

94

*a blanket and book will set the stage for the distance
I guess I need to feel.*

*Not from you, Mom! I could hear you taking
that personally, but don't. I just mean away from
people. Just a few hours with my pony, Troy, and
maybe a nap over Nancy Drew or something?
Please don't worry, I'll call before six if I'm not
already home by then.*

Love, Laura

I spent the night at the most outrageous party ever,
and Mom sat quietly at home, imagining me wrapped
in the words of a good book, sinking softly into a
blanket on the grass. I'll need to make sure Troy gets a
ride tonight . . . somehow . . . shit. I hadn't thought of
him until now . . . I hope Zippy doesn't phone to
suggest he take Troy out . . . damn. I'll be right back.
I'm going to ring the stables right away.

So! Bobby had borrowed his uncle's truck for the
night, and as long as we stayed on the 21 we weren't
running the risk of getting pulled over . . . Bobby
without a license . . . me no sleep, and an enormous
lie, in my book, to my parents . . .? Can you imagine?

Off we went, music playing surprisingly loud and
clear for the age of the truck . . . it made me feel like it
all worked. The way the trees were blowing, the speed
of the truck, the music, my nerves as I began to
undress into my birthday gift, sent via air mail from
Cousin Maddy. Did I even tell you, I talked to her for
almost an hour last week? Well, this dress is to die for,
skin tight, and it came with an insert in the breast area
that allowed you, if you so desired, to lift your breasts
upwards, instead of leaving them flat the way some

dresses do. Bobby nearly killed us, when he missed a tree by a quarter inch. He said it would have been worth it to die, 'with my eyes transfixed on a bosom as sweet as yours'. Doesn't that sound like a country song or something . . . transfixed on a bosom as sweet as yours . . .?

Bobby took me off to the side of the truck before we went into the house. He kissed me, and then said it was important that I knew that Leo, from a straw's distance, is a great guy, funny and can hold his own in a chat. Then he shook his head in a drastic 'N.O.' I wanted to know what the hell that meant, I mean what if I did what he said N.O. to? Bobby turned around just when we got in the doorway, and he said, 'Tonight it's not important, I'm pretty sure you'll hang with me . . . just don't ever fuck the guy. He's into some weird shit, that Leo, man . . .' I nodded and was suddenly, unmistakably intrigued by the phrase 'weird shit' and its sexual context. Bobby went to grab me a beer, I guess, and Leo came up to me. Shit . . . it was there, right away.

Both of us knew it, and he said, 'Laura Palmer . . . how 'bout that? Last time I saw you, Old Dwayne Milford was giving you a plaque or something . . . some prize you won . . .?' I had to interrupt him –

'*Finest Performance/Five Consecutive Years.*'

He asked if I had proof of performance quality, and I assured him proof was in abundance but I was about to fall asleep and die of thirst at the same time. He called to Bobby, which I was grateful for, seeing as how I was entering a bedroom, post warning and all.

(Hang on, I gotta do a couple of lines . . . I'm coming down and I'm about to tell you some incredible stuff – hang on.) So I'm in this room with Leo and

Bobby, and just as we're about to pass the straw, the door to a bathroom opens. A bathroom off the bedroom . . . and Ronnette Pulaski walked out of it, looking like she had given up junk food, and had started taking pretty good care of everything on her body except her nose. She was pretty high, and just the way Leo nodded his head toward her and said a quick hey led me to believe this was a regular kind of thing.

You want to hear something freaky? It didn't become completely clear to me until now, but when I went down to the spot BOB takes me . . . and I was saying that sometimes I smelled my panties and wanted to put my face between the legs of a girl and taste her . . . (*God, sometimes it feels right to say, other times I can't*)? Well, I had actually just for that moment thought of Ronnette, just because she was the only girl aside from Donna that I had seen naked . . . we were in an assembly together about two years ago, maybe more, and we were the only two costume changes in the middle of the program . . . we changed clothes . . . and kind of smiled at one another . . . I guess I was attracted to her somehow . . . by the way her eyes appeared sad, but cold. I liked her body . . . anyway, it was strange to see her there. I have no idea what she thinks of me . . . I doubt it's wise to ask. All I need are rumors buzzing around that Ronnette and I are 'seeing' each other every chance we get. Mom would have to be sent to the Haywards', if not the hospital itself, and Dad, he'd most likely think we were talking about a new game . . . an extension of kick the can, maybe? Who cares . . .!!!

God, I am so high, I can't stop writing like a thousand words a minute. I hope for your sake that this is legible, because, Lord knows, I am in no space to slow down. This is the drug I have been waiting for all of my life! I feel strong, confident, sexy, intelligent, pretty fuckin' cool, I have to say, and not one person last night made mention of my age. I can hold my fuckin' own . . . I could feel the vibes when we walked in.

I knew it was going to be one of those, Bobby was right, parties. Fucking crazy stuff goin' on in the corner or something. Leo was watching with basically 100 per cent concentration, so Bobby and I had to go see.

Man, there was this chick, lying with her skirt pulled up, and she was bettin' that no one could get her off . . . and if they did, it was a hundred big ones. She was asking five to give it a shot.

Now remember, I had been at the party for a fair amount of time, and I was pretty fixed up as far as being sedated and wired simultaneously . . . I looked around at everyone, and I must have been showing it all across my face, because Bobby pulled me back a bit by the arm, and I said I wanted to try it, if it didn't make him too uncomfortable, and he just looked at me like there was no changing my mind now anyway . . . so . . . I don't think he thought I would ever even consider such things . . .

I asked if I could speak privately in her ear . . . before making a decision, and she said she'd love to hear my voice up close . . . so I leaned in, and I said I'm going to make you feel real good . . . That hundred bucks is already spent . . .

I looked up for a moment, and I asked if she was relaxed. She said she was already getting a strange feeling that I knew what I was doing . . . I made her move a little on the couch, and I kissed her, just a soft kiss, on her lips . . .

Before I had even touched her she wanted me to know her name . . . I told her I'd call her what she needed to hear. She was beginning to get me pretty hot, which I didn't think would happen . . . but it helped, because the feelings just worked together . . . just clicked.

I opened her and I told her she was pretty, did she know that? She nodded. I told her I couldn't hear what she had said . . . She said YES! I smiled . . . 'Yes, what?' I said. 'I didn't hear you . . .'

She took a long breath and she brought her fingers to her mouth, and the guys behind her starting goin' 'Yeah.'

I heard someone in the back drop his glass, and he said, 'Shit, man, this girl is gettin' her to do it . . . she's even askin' for it, man . . .'

I knew she wanted to say things. I made sure she had to ask, yell something . . . I knew she wanted to hear that . . . for the men in the room to hear it. I told her everyone was looking at her. I told her they all could feel and taste it with their eyes . . . some men moved their fingers to let out the heat in their hands. I knew it was happening for her, I just had to keep her safe . . . she wanted it bad, and I told her she was beautiful. Boom! She was grabbing at me . . . pulling my hair . . . calling, 'Laura, Laura . . . God, the way you make me feel . . .!'

This big guy was trying to squeeze his way in, and I told him to back off a minute . . . he was bent out of shape, but then watched how desperately the girl needed just a moment to herself.

She took me by the hair and she said, 'I haven't been able to do that for almost two years . . . I'd like to see you back here, if I haven't scared you off already.'

It dawned on me that it was an appropriate time to mention that I felt like I was coming down a little, maybe from the sugar kisses . . . This guy came up to me, and he looked at me, straight in the eye.

'Little one.' He waited. 'I just had to come look at you, see your skin and all.' He smiled. 'I never saw so many guys go from lookin' at her like she was nothing to wishing they were you.'

I told him I was glad he liked it . . . I didn't mean to break up the party, the way I did . . . I have a hard time believing I did it . . . I guess I'm sort of out of my mind . . . I guess they left because I went a little . . .

He laughed and said, 'No one's going anywhere except outside on the lawn with a picture of you floatin' through their heads . . . They'll be back soon as they all empty out.'

The woman finally made it up off the couch and came and kissed my chest, where the dress cut low at the neck . . .

She wanted me to know she felt she owed me one if we ever crossed paths again . . .

Leo let me know that I made his party. Guys will be talking for a while 'bout this . . .

Talk about a weird way to meet people.

I'm going to have to visit Leo soon and see how many of my thoughts strike him . . . Maybe he'll do some of those weird things that Bobby warned me about . . . I'll bet I freaked Bobby out tonight anyway . . . I can't understand what got into me, but I wanted it . . . I wanted to try and there it was.

I don't care how high I am or how high I was . . . It felt good doing all of it. You can bet I'll do it again.

Laura

I dreamed about BOB last night. Not a real nice dream at all, a little sick in my opinion because I have so much hatred for the way he spoiled me . . . made me feel ugly and bad for wanting love or affection . . . He ruined all of my pride and self-esteem for the longest time . . . I could only be pretty and sweet, because pretty and sweet was easy . . . good grades even better. No one wanted me . . . I wouldn't even let on that I knew what sex was.

He did ruin me, didn't he? I mean, in the dream he came to the window at Leo's and saw me. It was a nastier scene in the dream than it was last night in reality. He kept showing this image of me again and again.

And then he was standing by the tree and he said, *'YOU WOULDN'T HAVE BEEN ABLE TO DO ANY OF THAT IF IT WEREN'T FOR ME.'*

I told him he was wrong. I told him I learned all that he saw when I was alone, so that I could do something to make myself feel good and be able to heal the wounds that he made.

He said, *'OH, YEAH, THEN WHY DO YOU WANT LEO TO TIE YOU UP, MAYBE EAT YOU THAT WAY, MAKE YOU A SLAVE? I KNOW YOU WANT IT . . . JUST THE WAY I TAUGHT YOU, LITTLE BITCH. I SAW YOU WITH THE WAND, PLAYING WITH YOURSELF . . . YOU WERE THINKING OF BAD BOY LEO, NOT BOBBY LITTLE BOY WHO WEEPS AFTER HE GETS FUCKED BY A LITTLE SLUT LIKE YOU.'*

And I woke up. Ashamed. Horrified. Guilty. And I imagined him suddenly, right before me at the edge of my bed.

YOU FORGOT, LAURA, I KNOW EVERYTHING, SEE EVERYTHING, GO ANYWHERE I WANT ... I COULD TELL YOU MORE ABOUT WHAT YOU THINK ARE SECRETS THAN YOU COULD TELL YOURSELF! YOU LET YOUR GUARD DOWN, DIDN'T YOU? LET ME HAVE A NICE VACATION FROM THAT STENCH OF YOURS ... THEN YOU HAD TO CALL ME BACK ... RANCID LITTLE BITCH! YOU'RE PRETTY MEAN TO ME SOMETIMES WHEN YOU WRITE, AREN'T YOU? WE'LL HAVE TO FIX THAT. MAKE YOU LOVE ME LIKE YOU USED TO. I REMEMBER THAT ... SOON YOU WILL TOO.

And then he disappeared. I need to do something that is right and good, *today*!

Who in the fuck is he and why does he hate me so much?

I want to die, and to forget everything else. I can't take it any more! I begin to feel good and then someone makes me feel that I'm dirty. Then someone kisses me just right and I feel wanted and excited all over again.

I need to know if what I'm doing is right. I can't let BOB be the one who taught me to wish to be tied up sometimes.

I don't ever want to be hurt. I never have. I only want to play the games where I have to say dirty things sometimes, not mean things like BOB thinks, and if I am punished, I am punished with sex, not pain.

BOB is not who puts these ideas in my head. I won't let him be the one. These are my private thoughts.

I'm afraid I'll never make it in and out of another sexual experience, ever, without being afraid he will come and tell everyone lies about me.

If someone who loves me reads this years from now, please try not to hate me. I only feel the way I feel. I don't hurt anyone else, and I don't want to. I try every day to be better and more the way I think the world wants to see a girl like me.

But I am Laura. I am sad. God, I'm sad again! Why? I miss laughter and a day where time is spent with my friends who don't care what I think of late at night. They don't hate me for sometimes dreaming late at night, with my hand buried between my legs, ashamed, and of how I wish that my other hand would simply pull the trigger.

BOB, I forbid you to come to me ever again, in dreams or in reality. You are not welcome! *I hate you.*

I feel so alone, Laura

I tried to talk to Dad at breakfast and he just sat there twitching, like he doesn't have time for any extra thoughts. Doesn't have time for the fucking suicide dreams his own daughter is having. Neither one of my parents will talk to me . . . What is this? *Some kind of a dream?*

Dad took off all of his clothes and shouted, 'It's a dream . . . Fucking relax, would you? . . . So your mother saw photos of you licking the little privates of other women. It appeared in these photos that you were enjoying yourself. Is this true?'

I've never been more afraid than I am this very minute.

I didn't even realize I was sleeping when that was written . . . was I?

Shit, this is too weird. Just a little too weird.

Was BOB here? Was BOB inside . . . ?

I won't even think it.

                                                            L

Dear Diary, February 3, 1987

There is no cocaine. It's gone. I hate the way I feel
. . . so much like I've been in a vacuum, my body has
been violated, my thoughts, my dreams, the images I
have of Mom and Dad are now awful and depressing
pictures I can't stop seeing . . . Oh, if she ever knew
the things that have happened.

I wonder if anyone would believe me if I told them
all I know about him . . . I could have the police wait
for him, until he showed up, but he would know just
like he knows everything in my mind. My mind is his
toy. Something he bats around, with his paws. I'm
just going to have to tell everyone and make them
believe. And just tell . . .

*TELL THEM WHAT, LAURA PALMER? TELL
THEM THAT I TAKE YOU AWAY AND YOU
NEVER ARGUE? YOU NEVER SCREAM FOR
HELP? TELL THEM YOU SEE ME BUT NO
ONE ELSE DOES? NO ONE WILL BELIEVE
YOU, LAURA PALMER . . . I'M TOO CARE-
FUL.*

Dear God . . . it's happened again . . . He's stepped
on to the page . . . This is not at all what I was trying
to write! It frightens me terribly to know that BOB
found his way into the pages of my diary as if he were
feeding the words to my mind, just seconds in time for
me to think that they are my own.

Is there something I can get for you, BOB . . .
anything the family might own that you would take in
trade for your permanent absence?

Talk to me, BOB . . . about a trade . . . trade me for something else.

I AGREE. I'LL TRADE.

Who will it be?

CAN'T TELL WITH THESE THINGS. . . . I MAY CHANGE MY MIND.

I thought so.

L

I need coke, bad, or I'll never make it.

I gotta reach Bobby. Where the fuck is he when I need him? This is just great. I'm here, Laura Palmer, honor student, model citizen of Twin Peaks ... and I've got a habit I've only just begun.

I'm not ready for this job ... I'm still afraid BOB's waiting.

If he's in the woods he'll get me now, 'cause fuck if I don't plan on having a big fat line of confidence up my nose in about half an hour. A big white line that calls my name the way a lover should. I wish BOB would trade. If he goes, I'll try and find the person and tell them to beware *OF THE MAN WHO CAN SLIP MAYBE IN AND OUT OF YOU LIKE A WIND THAT GOES UNNOTICED, THEN CREEPS UP ON YOU AND SHOVES A FIST INTO THE WOMAN SPACE YOU SEEM TO HAVE FALLEN SO IN LOVE WITH, LAURA PALMER ... YOU SHOULDN'T WISH FOR THINGS ... YOU WON'T GET WHAT YOU WANT, I'LL MAKE SURE OF IT.*

REMEMBER, LAURA PALMER, I CAN MANIPULATE YOUR CONSCIENCE SO THAT YOU FEEL NOTHING BUT WHAT I CHOOSE FOR YOU TO FEEL. DON'T YOU FEEL LIKE DYING, LAURA PALMER? DON'T YOU JUST FEEL LIKE GIVING IN TO ME AGAIN? TAKE ME BACK AND I WON'T CAUSE A HORRIBLE ACCIDENT LATER TODAY. IF SOMEONE GETS HURT, YOU CAN SMILE KNOWING IT'S ALL DUE TO YOU. SELFISH, DRUG ADDICT LESBIAN!

Fuck you!

Maybe if I just get to Leo's for some coke, I can get my shit together and earn my freedom back. My privacy of thought, all of it. I'm taking it back. It belongs to me. I just need some coke ... I need a ride out of here ... Fuck it, I'll walk. I'll just get up walk downstairs and out the front door like nothing is wrong. I'll get some coke and everything will be better. I will be able to think. I'll just walk to Leo's and everything will be fine.

I'll bring you with me, Diary –
Laura

Dear Diary,   April 2, 1987

Leo had company of the female persuasion, and they were unable to get to the door.

Oh, God . . . money . . . shit! Maybe he'll front the coke to me, and I can pay him later, or . . . wait, he's coming out of the house.

Talk soon, L

Leo will be fair about the coke money, I hope I hope I hope.

He's got it, and it's good. He just set me up with a noseload . . . and my head is starting to sort through the mental files again . . . feel the blood in my veins . . . I told Leo I wasn't like this weird addict, but I just haven't slept in so long . . . Wait!

BOB is gone. I can't feel him around. Maybe it's because I'm high. Maybe I'm crazy and I made him up . . . No, fuck that. I'm crazy if I believe he's only in my imagination . . . he's real. I know he's real. I do. I couldn't and wouldn't create something as evil as the man.I speak of.

I am beginning to truly become what BOB told me I would. A fallen girl, misused, mistrusted, lost, loves sex and drugs because they are always there, making me feel the high I expect . . . no surprises. Can't you see you're killing me, BOB? Is that the point?

I miss the days only a year or so ago when I could hardly remember a thing . . . I just knew somehow that on certain nights I came home, cried a lot, and hid behind the bathroom door, ashamed. I remember what you said to me, you shit! I remember! I know you cut me when I was very young, several times, and you told me that I was in big trouble because I had bled. You told me good children don't bleed down their legs. You told me I was not a child of God! Was there anything you chose to allow me to feel normal about? I grew up with you always there, showing me evidence of my evil blood and nature. You were that voice . . . you son of a bitch.

Leo needs to see me about money . . . I hope this transaction goes smoothly, painlessly, and silently. I told Leo that if Bobby shows up, I need to hear from him right away.

We've got to find another dealer just for tonight . . . I got the last of the pure, except for Leo's personal stash, and that's just what the name says. Personal. If I didn't have so much shit on my mind, I wouldn't need more than this for the night, but I do. I have to have it. It's all I have right now, man. My friend, the white line, who I am so conveniently reminded of each time I travel a major highway or see a snowstorm or a dash of baby powder, sitting like a tease inside my own fucking house.

I hope we can get more. We have to. After the past few days without sleep, this fuckin' BOB deal . . . I just can't go to sleep. Too dangerous.

AND WHAT, LAURA PALMER, IT'S BEEN TWO, THREE DAYS SINCE YOU FIRST SNORTED . . . YOU ARE A MESSED-UP BITCH . . . STILL HERE.

Fuck you, BOB. So I am what you always told me I was. A little bitch, dirty and sleazy and fucking poeple to pay for drugs. You win. You fed me pain when I had none, and when I did have pain, you said it was my own fault . . . I think you are the most repulsive, evil, conniving man ever to set foot in my life, where you had no invitation, no right. What in the fuck do you want! You cheat by never ever having to argue with someone strong enough to fight you . . . Conquer someone like that, then I'll admit you've won. I'll even follow you. No arguments.

Laura Palmer believes you are a cheat.

L

It is very late at night and I do not care to check in or to alert someone of where I am or even if I am safe. I don't care to think about it. I don't want to know any more about myself, from anyone . . . too many lies have entered me, like bullets that made wounds . . . slow bleeding. It would be years later that I would notice. Begin to feel the weakness. Fall into the world of drugs. The world of sex for show and power. For strength I thought I wanted, I went to the wrong people.

The part of me with the ability to decide for myself whether something is right or wrong has been taken away. A decision lasts only a moment for me before I doubt it and curse myself for ever thinking I was capable of choosing right over wrong . . . I should have learned ages ago how to remember you. Perhaps I could have saved myself some very sad moments . . . very bad dreams, and several hundred desperate attempts at regaining my better self. The one who welcomed you in. The one to whom you owe an entire lifetime.

I certainly hope you got what you needed.

I can't have good things, not now. I don't know the road to responsibility, the way I used to. So simple to just walk down . . .

I have sent Troy away. Set him free with several lashes to the ass (a method that kept me running for some time, as you must remember, BOB).

He's gone. I don't deserve him, nor does he deserve a life that begins and ends each day in a small square box. A reminder, if you will, that he is not free, but owned.

I let the pony go. One of the last things I had hoped for before recalling all of your . . . shit. It doesn't matter anyway.

I hope Troy understood why I made him leave me.

I'm so afraid that anything I touch runs the risk of contact with BOB. I'll be investigating death . . . don't worry. I can feel you deciding how and when. You bastard

                                                    Laura

Dear Diary, November 12, 1987

I hope God reads this: I could use the help.

It is definitely the end of my life, the end of my belief in myself . . . trust . . . everything gone! Leo and Bobby came to get me at the stables because I could hardly walk another step. Bobby said he had called home for me and told them he was taking me out to a surprise dinner . . . we'd be back late.

That was sweet and very considerate of him, I must admit. But like I told Leo and Bobby from the backseat as I changed clothes (again a thank-you to Bobby for borrowing something for me to wear of Donna's – who tells Bobby she is worried about me). I'll admit surprises here, not that I doubt Donna's loyalty or her friendship, but I believe now too much in BOB. I told them both that I was worried. That I had good reason not to leave any one place, all night long. I said I was concerned enough that, if we all agreed, we could turn back and forget the coke until tomorrow. Bobby laughed at me, and Leo patted my hand as if I were something cute, something that chirped the same message again and again. Pulling a string at my back, unnecessary. 'I don't think this is very safe.'

We drove out past Mill Town and deeper into Low Town. I've never seen a night so dark. No moon anywhere in the sky. This even worried Leo, who I'm sure will take good care of me, until I go. Everything I need right now is either a substance or the cash with which to buy a substance. My little white friend. Another lie, but at least I looked this one right in the face and said I'd believe it anyway. Temporary happiness is better than slowly allowing friends, family, lovers, a frightening peek at how close I am to self-destructing. Don't come too close, there is no longer safety in numbers. I can promise you that.

We drove up to a small road without a posted sign of any kind, but assumed it was the right road, as it was the only one around for miles. Bobby just sat there before driving down toward the house. Leo egged him on, like, 'C'mon, Bobby, let's drive.' I tried to get his attention, too, but he was honestly in another world. His face was something out of the Twilight Zone.

The minute Bobby came out of his thought he began barreling down the road, complete darkness ahead of us that somewhere shadowed a house. One I hoped was filled to an obscene level with cocaine and a quick drink if I managed a smile ... Show teeth, I thought.

Leo looked at me like for a moment it struck him as wrong to be down here, under these conditions, not knowing anyone, and padded up with cash totaling in the thousands. I just slid back into my seat and shut up, suddenly realizing how ridiculous it was of me to change clothes ... I'm only dressed for trouble when it comes to Low Town in an hour of darkness still not explained in news reports or radio stations. They're not even saying there is a power failure.

I said, 'I wonder, how long would it take the police to get down here after a call?'

Bobby reached into his jacket and produced his father's pistol. It gleamed only slightly and I told him he was completely fucked out of his mind to be carrying that around with him. I was now sure that it was not a stomach ache I was experiencing, but instead a quite obvious gut instinct to turn around and drive like fuck-all until we were close to home.

The car did not turn, nor did it slow. The road showed no signs of life, no house up ahead, not a fucking soul around . . . well, perhaps a soul or two . . . which was even more reason to make a silent getaway while we still had the chance to leave together.

Out of nowhere, it seemed, Bobby slammed on the brakes. The truck spun in two full circles and dust shot up and began to glow in the light from the headlights. Finally we stopped. We were all in a bit of shock. 'I thought I saw someone,' Bobby said. 'I didn't want to run him over.' We all got out and moved slowly in the dark.

All of a sudden someone grabbed me from behind and began to strangle me. I thought, I don't believe I'm going to die this way . . . in Low Town during a blackout no one will even admit is actually going on while I'm trying to buy drugs, cocaine to be specific, and neither of the two strong and burly men I have as companions know I'm being fucking strangled! I thought that was it . . . I'd bought the goddamn farm here. Cash. Paid in full.

The grip loosened, my vision blurred and I passed out cold.

I woke up in this drug dealer's house with a headache that thought it was an aneurism. Bobby and Leo came into the room, and Bobby obediently took a seat next to me and acted worried about my head, and his concern reminded me of just how it had happened. And I said (a fair amount of sarcasm in this, I might add), 'Whose fuckin' bright idea was it to strangle me until I passed out cold?'

No one responded.

'Then I guess this would be the way you guys meet chicks here in Low Town?' Silence in return. 'Classy.'

The fattest of the four dudes pulled a gun from his shirt and aimed it at me. I looked at him, like he was going a bit overboard maybe . . . that a 'Shut up' or 'Fuck off' would have been perfectly clear to me. He cocked the mother-fuckin' thing and brought it to my face.

'I apologize, sweetheart. Can't expect everyone wearing a dress to be a girl.' He looked at me, licked his gun. 'Nice titties.'

'I know.' Not that his explanation for strangling me made any sense at all. His apology was accepted, and quite seriously preferred over a permanent hole in my head. I offered my hand and thanked him for not shooting me. It would have really fucked up my evening. There was a pause . . . and no handshake.

Slowly, and with great pleasure, he began to curl the edges of his mouth up up up, and ended the performance in a frozen 'eat shit and die' grin, the likes of which I had only seen once before. I knew the deal was bogus. I found myself kept alert and up to date on the etiquette of silence by the four pistols that found quite important parts of my face on which to rest their barrels.

Cold metal. A chill at the base of my neck. Frightening. Call me crazy, but weapons often cause me to hyperventilate and desire large quantities of fresh air ASAP.

I told them I was going to the truck. I kept thinking one of the guns would go off and make a beeline for me. I had to get air, which was made more difficult than usual due to the shrinkage that took place in my neck. Besides, I'm afraid of bullets and would bet good money that they hurt when inserted inside the flesh at a high speed.

I was suddenly aware of persons in military attire, posted like frozen nightmares all around the house. One of the soldiers came up to my window and I was all huddled up because it was chilly and I was frightened.

With one of the straightest faces I had ever seen, he asked, 'You ever think about dying?'

'Not in a situation like this one. No, sir.'

He looked at me like I had just made his promotion arrive a few days earlier than scheduled, and he said, 'You want to step outside the vehicle, please, miss.'

'Are you just going to shoot me or something?'

'There's been a fair amount of cocaine stolen from inside the house. I thought maybe you'd like to show me that the truck is clean and we can go on with business . . . per the norm.'

I got out and I thought I was going to shatter into little pieces of bone, I was so scared. 'Everything okay?'

'On my end of the shotgun, yes, it is.'

I couldn't move.

'Your end isn't much of a party, is it?'

'No. No, it's more like a wake . . . no party I'd like to go to. Sir.'

'You can go on back to your seat and relax.'

'What's going on in the house, right now?'

He shrugged. 'I guess the boys are sitting around debating whether or not to blow their faces off or send 'em back to High Town just the way they came in.'

'Oh. I feel much more relaxed now. Thank you.'

I had to sit in that fuckin' truck for almost forty minutes waiting to find out if Bobby and Leo were allowed to drive home in solid, rather than liquid, form. At last, they came out of the front door patting these bullies on the backs and laughing like they went way back. I thought, gee, this is great. I'm out here about to be shot point-blank for lifting a kilo of cocaine (I carefully inserted it under my dress, which still appeared skintight, and proved me innocent of the theft), and the thanks I get is a snail's pace on the way to the truck. And a cheesy example of male bonding if I ever saw one.

And then a look of total fear came from Bobby's eyes to mine and registered, 'Look out!' Guns started going off like the NRA had accepted applicants who were legally blind. People were just fucking shooting at each other . . . paranoid, and so high that if they were hit, they'd notice some time tomorrow.

I slid over into the driver's seat and swung around to where Leo was hiding, unarmed, praying like a madman, and we were gone speeding down the road back toward the city.

Then, it was my turn to send the 'Oh shit' look. When we were halfway down the road, I looked in the rearview mirror and saw someone else in the truck bed with Leo, and Leo was losing something awful. Bobby pulled out his gun and with his free hand, lifted himself out of the side window and told the guy he had two seconds to disappear or die. He had to choose fast . . .

The guy sat up, and *Bobby shot him in the chest at a range of about three, maybe four feet*. The speed of the bullet sent the guy flying out of the back of the truck and on to the ground behind us. Bobby screamed at me, 'Get the hell outa' here. *Drive!*'

As soon as we were back on paved roads, Bobby lowered himself into the cab, still holding the gun in his hand as if he were ready to fire.

Bobby was silent the whole way home. Leo sat in back and thanked God for the miracle of prayer. I wondered if there was a lot of blood in the back of the truck, and if the man was dead . . .

At Leo's house I walked in and asked him if we were alone. He said we were, and so I removed the entire kilo of cocaine from my skirt, plastic in mint condition. A good job, I thought, for an amateur like myself. I apologized to Bobby for probably causing the extra man to hide in back.

I was searched, though, and the guy said I was clean. I thought they'd given up, seeing as how everyone was hugging each other on the way out of the house.

'They were telling us nice and slow,' Leo said, 'how they'd find us and remove our genitalia a half inch at a time . . . with a butter knife. If the bimbo with us was sitting on a kilo of their coke, it wouldn't be long before we'd bypass all hospitals and go directly to hell.'

I sat down and thought for a moment about the word 'bimbo'.

'Hey, you guys,' I said. 'I'm real sorry. I wouldn't have done it if I didn't think you guys would be jumping up and down about it.'

No response.

'I'm the one who suggested we not go at all, remember?'

A smile from both of them.

Leo nodded toward the kilo and said, 'You got yourself quite a party in that bag.'

Bobby turned and looked at me with sudden pride. 'A coupla regular Bonnie and Clydes.'

That drama ended and yet there was another to

come. We, of course, decided to begin blowing the stuff up our noses in quantities never before accepted by the human body. If the bullets didn't kill us, the mountain of cocaine would come in a close second.

We were high. I needed to get out. I wanted some stuff from the Cash and Carry. Neither of them would even think of leaving the couch. They were into the television, and even more so the macho thrill of sitting in front of a mountain of cocaine, with three straws protruding from a hole at the top of the bag.

Both of them looked at me with puppy-dog eyes and dilated pupils and said, 'Do you mind if we just hang?' I was a little pissed at Bobby for not offering to escort his own girlfriend, the very one who had risked her life, however worthless at the moment, to ensure that he be as high as he was.

I figured screw 'em and decided I could handle a two-block drive down the road to the store, without breaking into the sweats or experiencing an emotional breakdown.

I drove off, and as I passed the only two other homes on the road, I noticed a magazine lying on the floor of the truck that I hadn't noticed earlier. *Fleshworld Magazine*.

My mind went reeling, a magazine that could perhaps teach me something I hadn't thought of myself . . . and BAM!

I pulled over to the side of the road, and before I got out of the truck to see what I had hit, I saw myself four years ago. A young girl, awakened by the noise, came flying from the front door and began to slow as she saw the animal in the road.

She looked at it and took one step closer, still not going within fifteen feet of it, as if to spare herself the reality.

I turned and saw Jupiter. A cat identical to the one I considered a best friend before some drughead like myself came along and, without any thought, cared more for the stories in a porn magazine than for what might be crossing the road.

I couldn't help but begin to cry. Then I couldn't stop. I was the person, years later, I had hated for taking my cat away from me when I needed his company the most. I told the little girl I would do whatever she thought was best. If she wanted a new cat, I would be happy to buy it . . . She looked at me – *and tried to cheer me up!* Her cat is stuck to the road because of my sex hang-ups, and she's trying to make me feel better.

She came around to the side of the truck, where I was leaning. I was unable to face her.

I felt such tremendous shame, I could barely move.
'Please, stop crying.'

Jesus, she even sounded like me.

'Why are you so sad? I didn't mean to make you feel so bad.'

I looked down at her and saw something I missed so much. Such a willingness to forgive. Such a big heart; this one girl could love all of these United States and leave no one feeling lonely.

'When I was just about your age, I had a cat who looked just like yours. I called him Jupiter, and he was probably the best friend around. Someone hit him out in the street, and I heard the noise and came running to help him. I remember I was so amazed by how quickly . . . death decides it is hungry.'

There was a moment when there was only wind. We said nothing.

Then she looked up at me and asked, 'Did you forgive the person who hit your cat?'

I crouched down beside her and told her that Jupiter was killed by someone who hit and ran. 'I figured he was in heaven, but I missed him a lot ... and I forgave his death, but I don't think I ever forgot that someone hit my cat, but didn't stop to say they were sorry.'

She held up her hand, and her nightgown, flannel, made me smile. 'My name is Danielle.' She shook my hand tight.

'My name is Laura Palmer.' I gave her a hug and she wrapped her arms around me, warm. 'It's very nice to meet you, Danielle.' I stood. 'It takes an awfully special person to forgive so easily.'

She held my hand for a minute, and after thinking about something very carefully she looked up at me and said, 'When I heard the noise, I was worried that the cat had been hurt ... But I came out, and I saw you, and you were crying more than me, because you remembered your cat, and it made you sorry you hurt this one. Why would I want to make you feel bad for anything you do? I think you're nice, Laura Palmer.'

'Danielle, I think you are extra special nice, with sugar on top.' I looked away toward the cat, then back to her.

'My mom is gonna get it.'

Little Danielle made me feel, more than anyone I had been around in ages, that there was still a chance for everything to work out. I even began to think a new cat would be nice ...

I just remembered that I set my horse free. I hope I didn't send him off somewhere where he might be hit, or not taken care of the way he should. I guess I should have thought of that before I allowed myself to be swept away by the drama of setting my horse free, to go and do whatever he wished ... Alone.

Boy, I'm not racking up the brownie points this week, am I? What very dark but almost omenlike events I've gone through. Why?

Am I supposed to get back up on to life and get a job? Or am I still revved up to die? All I know is I'm taking the truck back right away, and I'm leaving the drugs behind for a sobering walk home. Maybe Mom will make hot chocolate, and I can edit the evening's events and just be with my mom.

I'll just take the truck back and go right home. I'll just walk. Just get home.

Write you when we get there.

L

I am home. It's early. Leo and Bobby weren't very happy about the fact that I wanted to go home. Leo had decided that it was going to be a night of new and 'unusual' things. Bobby was really, really high, and I think Leo had told him that he was supposed to talk me into going along with whatever Leo wanted, because I had never seen him so concerned about keeping me somewhere. His constant looks toward Leo made me think Bobby felt guilty, or maybe uncertain about whether or not he should be leading me into this. Waving the cheese in front of the mouse . . . a blond-haired, very frightened, little mouse. See the trap? See it? Go. You wanted this anyway, remember?

Leo shook his head when I told them I had decided I wanted to leave, that something had happened that made me feel . . . I stopped. I didn't finish my sentence because I suddenly saw that the two of them were in no position even to pretend they cared about some cat out on the road. An animal in white, perhaps still there . . . or like I imagined it while driving slow, lights off, back to the end of the road. I saw its dead eyes locking on the vision of a mother, probably tired and wondering if her daughter would be all right. Wondered, as she carefully lifted the animal's body, if death stopped right here. Maybe she thought about work to be done the next day, thought about hovering there in the road . . . so tired, always tired.

I guess I'm thinking of myself here. I am tired. I'm the one who asks, is death only the frozen image we have of the animal's body? Grandfather's ashes, just an easier way to fit him inside an urn? He's just a body anyway: why not decorate the remains?

When I die, I guess they'll bury me. I hope the cat was buried. I thought of staying there to help, but everything was too close. The body there like a message.

Maybe roadkills are more than they seem. Messages, like tonight's was . . . or examples we never pay attention to. This is what it is. Stillness. Eternal privacy. I didn't want to stay tonight with the guys. I wanted to go home, sleep in my bed, be a little girl again. Fake an illness or cramps and ask Mom to take care of me. Read *Sleeping Beauty* or *Stuart Little*, sip coffee while she turns pages, watches me.

I wanted that, but I knew I would end up staying at the house. Sneak in early, before dawn . . . beat the alarm by seconds. Strip down to nothing and slip into bed. I knew I'd tell you what happened. Simply. With a pen, and no sound. Words have been strange to me these past few days. Mine have been lies, again and again. Another comes along to help the other lie live . . . stay real. Bobby's words have been like little knives. I know he doesn't mean to hurt me, but his surprise in my behavior, the other night, last night, the difference he sees when I get high . . . and there's been a lot of that. He says he never knew I was so wild inside. I think he means that he never knew I was so bad. He never knew Laura Palmer the way the woods, the trees, the earth, knew her. Often shaken and angry, threatened, paralyzed, unable to run. Or never chose to. Laura Palmer was told that she deserves pain, and a kind of closeness most people never talk or think about because they think it's wrong. Laura Palmer? She was born without a choice. Was told very quietly, one night long ago, that she would like it, or she would have to be killed.

126

I stayed at the house. Leo wanted me to drink something. Relax. He said he wanted me the way I had been. He said I had promised him. He'd make sure I was home in time . . . no one would know. He kneeled down in front of me and took me by the wrists, tight. I thought of BOB and closed my eyes. I must have winced, made a sound, something, because he said, 'I knew it. I knew this meant something to you.' He moved his hold on me down to my hands. Held them more softly. 'Good. I knew you'd understand. I saw it.' I heard Bobby get up from his chair and I heard Leo stop him. 'Sit down, Bobby. Now. Laura will get you a drink. She'll open her eyes, and we'll all have a drink.'

I opened my eyes slowly. Leo let my hands rest in my lap. I stood up and went to the kitchen for Bobby's drink. I could hear the two of them talking in the other room. They started to argue about something. I think it was about me, the plans for the evening. It actually hurt my head, my ears, when they argued. I didn't want any more talking like that. I went out to where they were sitting and told them to shut up. I wanted them to shut up. I would do or say whatever tonight's 'games' required. There didn't need to be fighting. I wanted to have fun. I wanted to be high. High like they were. I wanted to forget what had happened outside on the road.

Bobby came into the kitchen and told me I was lucky Leo hadn't given me a good smack for telling him to shut up in his own house. I told him it wasn't luck. I knew Leo liked me. If he hit me, ever, it would be part of the agreement.

Bobby said that he'd like to go out, just the two of us, next week maybe, on a date. He missed being with

Laura. I hated him for saying that. I wanted to slap him. Instead, I told him I didn't miss Laura at all. I told him he may never see her again.

We drank for a long time just sitting there doing lines and watching Leo: I didn't know what for, but I knew I had to be ready. He might be nice, he might not. I wasn't looking at Bobby the whole time. I made sure he saw me with Leo. I didn't like Bobby's missing the sweet Laura. I can't wake her now. She doesn't like nights like this. She wouldn't want to play. I did. I needed to be someone different from her . . . I had to shake off whatever calls BOB to my window. Shake the scent of innocence. I decided something. I told them I wanted to go out, into the woods. Leo looked pleased and smiled at Bobby. He looked back at me, nodded toward my empty drink. 'You feelin' fucked up?' I told him I was, but I didn't want to be inside any more. I didn't like the light. I told him it made things too easy.

I started to pack up some coke for the woods, and Leo looked at me like I was stealing or something. I told him, 'Listen, I stole the shit, right? I'm the one that's going to make your night . . . and I am not going to start to come down while I'm out in the woods.' He said he was just watching me. Said I should relax. Then he came over to me, close. He said he liked it when I stood up for myself, but there would be no room for that out in the woods.

I suddenly pictured myself out in the darkness with my arms spinning me around, spinning, Leo and Bobby in my sight each time I spun . . . Then a slow dream of Leo, his eyes big, pleased, lips parting, his hands coming together again and again as he slowly applauded my performance.

Before we left, Bobby came out of the bathroom and said he'd decided he was tired, didn't want to be around. He said he knew that tonight was about Leo and me anyway. He said maybe he'd call me in a few days. Leo smiled as Bobby slammed the front door shut.

'Bobby's a smart boy.'

I nodded, but inside I wanted to kill Bobby for making me feel bad. He wanted Laura, sweet and pure, to run after him, walk home beside him, her hand in his. He made me want her for a moment. It wasn't safe. He didn't understand how unsafe that was for all of us, especially out here. The woods needed to see me tonight. They needed to see how I've grown, what I've become. Then they can tell BOB to stay away from me. He'll think his job with me is done.

Leo came over to me and slipped his hand up my blouse, held my eyes with his, found the nipple with his finger. Held my eyes, wouldn't let me look away, said, 'You won't miss him, you won't miss anyone.'

He released my eyes; my legs almost gave out on me. 'Take me somewhere, make me forget.' I reached for his arm so that I could regain my balance. He said he had something in mind. He said it could get scary, but it would be okay. He said if he liked me after tonight, we could really start to get close. He wanted to see me tonight first, alone.

He asked me if I liked to be scared.

I said that sometimes scary things happen, but they're gone in the morning. I told him I wanted to get really hot, I needed to feel that. I hadn't felt that for a long time. I had been busy giving it.

When we left the house, he put a blindfold around my head. He whispered, 'Can you feel the darkness?'

I told him I could.

He said, 'Good. I'm going to take you into it. Just like you wanted. I'll guide you, so you just walk with me until I tell you to stop.'

We began walking, and as we did, I felt the trees close in above me, noticed the wind, slowing, spinning until it settled, unable to return to the sky . . . I heard Leo breathe. Felt his hand on my back, strong. I wanted to tell him I was getting that feeling in my stomach. The one that makes you loose, makes you want things . . . But he wouldn't let me talk. He said that he would do all of the talking until he needed to know something from me. He was pretty sure, he said, that he would know how I felt without even hearing me say it.

It seemed like a long time before he stopped. And I didn't know what to do, so I waited. For his lead. When we finally came to a stop, I heard him begin to circle me, his footsteps faint on the needles covering the ground. I could feel his eyes as if they were hands, up and down, following this curve and that. He stopped behind me.

'Can you keep a secret, little girl?'

I wasn't sure if I should answer.

'It's okay. Go ahead and tell me.'

'Yes. I can keep a secret.'

I suddenly began to feel and smell the same deep musk of the woods. I know it well. I began to feel my fear setting in, and I had to roll my head, loosen up . . . fight it. Remember what this is about.

'The secret is that sometimes, right in this spot, I hear voices. Sometimes I realize that I'm not alone.'

'Whose voices do you hear?'

'The voices I don't know . . . But sometimes, if I am

very quiet, I find that I can feel these people around me. I can hear them talking about me, but if you were to try and see them, they would most definitely disappear.'

'Do you hear any voices now?'

'I think I hear them faintly. Coming in this direction. Does that scare you?'

'I don't think so, no.' I was ready for a busload of truckers to arrive and begin some kind of strange ceremony . . . I suddenly felt very exposed. I wondered how many people were on their way.

'I'm going to help you sit down. Over here.'

Leo sat me down and I realized I was in a quite comfortable chair, dead in the middle of the woods. What was this place? Had I ever seen it during the day? Music began to play. Strange sounds of water, and something I couldn't place . . . and a drum . . . low.

I felt it in my chest. It was loud enough that I was suddenly unable to sense by sound if someone was near me or not.

I heard in my ear, 'Wait here . . . relax. Enjoy.'

I'm not sure I can even describe to you the next five hours of time. The music was constant, a rhythm that made me sway and ache for more of everything. More of the hands that were suddenly upon me, lips soft along my neck, hands on my chest, thighs, face. Voices in my ears, whispering close . . . backing away.

I think that there were three different women, and at least four men, Leo included. I was tied, eventually, to the chair with a rope that bound my hands almost to the point of discomfort, which I knew was part of the game, and well planned. Each and every fantasy one might conjure late at night, with the exception of farm animals, was performed on, with, or for me. It was like I had been swallowed by a dream, perfect in every way. My only responsibility was to maintain my blindness and allow each person his chance to come and be with me.

I could hear them, the others who would wait in line to see me. Just voices in the woods, whose bodies became images I could hear, see them through the sounds they made . . . everything had become so sensitive. I could hear them all night as they would excite each other to the point of small internal convulsions, billions of tiny waves of light, water, electricity, running through them. All of them would react with a strange joy and amazement . . . a thirst when one would reach a climax. Even I, who sat away from them as if on display (more a trophy than a freak), felt pleasure in the sounds around my feet.

These people, all of various ages, spent evenings in the woods, forgetting names and histories, using only their most basic feelings and wishes to be held and touched, wanted, and completely accepted, no matter what they looked like, or who they were at work or school the following mornings. It was dark and strange and almost intoxicating at times. I would sway, my head heavy in this darkness. The energy was so thick, I almost felt the air separate, part slowly to let me move. Each and every nerve in my body had something to say . . . a scream beneath the skin, constant and much greater than usual because I could not sense it coming. I could swear there were times I was sensitive enough to feel the fingerprints of those who touched me. See them by how they felt across my skin . . . each pattern like light trails behind my eyes.

When I saw again, with my eyes, the image was of

my house. The light across it, just before sunrise . . . a yellow mist of light still fighting the shade that had not finished its stay.

It took me a minute to really focus. Leo sat next to me in his truck. He said he was leaving, and that his wife would be coming back home soon. In order to meet again, we would have to plan carefully. I had forgotten about the wife. Shelley. Quite pretty. She waitresses with Norma at the Double R. So, anyway, I told him to call me. He said he had a few things I'd be needing while he was away.

He handed me a backpack stuffed beyond its limit. He warned me not to open it until I was alone. He kissed me, then watched me go in the front door, and he drove off.

I had a daydream as I made my way upstairs that Mom woke up . . . and asked how the orgy had been. I gave her all the details and she began reliving her own experiences of strange evenings in the woods. She wanted to call her friends and tell them her daughter had been in an orgy . . . and wasn't that wonderful? The daydream ended when I reached the top of the stairs and saw that my bedroom door was wide open – I stopped dead in my tracks. I looked toward my parents' bedroom. The door was closed tight.

When I turned back to my room, what I saw was horrifying.

I could clearly see a man's shoe behind my door, and then he emerged, smiling. It was BOB. With one hand he took my wrist, and the other he placed across his lips, '*SHHHHHH*.' With one quick pull, he brought me inside the room with him. The door slammed shut behind me.

Stop. It must be a dream. I'm high. I haven't slept.

Don't wake Mom or Dad now or they'll know you've been out. They'll have questions you can't answer. Think.

I'm going crazy, pacing and struggling with thoughts, words, the image of that haunting grin. Stay away from me, BOB!

I CAN DO WHATEVER I WANT.

Stay away from this house! Leave me alone or I swear I'll find a way to make you sorry.

CAN'T FEEL SORRY, LAURA PALMER.

Look at where I am because of you, and your sickness, your weakness. You are an awful creature.

NO CONSCIENCE. NO GUILT. YOU SAID SO YOURSELF. I SEE YOU GOT YOURSELF FUCKED LAST NIGHT. AN OWL TOLD ME. REALLY INTO THAT COKE, AREN'T YOU? DIRTY GIRL, LAURA PALMER. YOU SHOULD KNOW BY NOW THAT YOU CAN'T IMPRESS ME . . . I'M NOT INTERESTED IN WHAT YOU DO WITH YOUR LITTLE COKE FRIENDS. YOU ALL LOOKED RIDICULOUS, OR SO I HEARD.

Get out of my head. Now!

NAH.

Leave me alone, you sick bastard. How dare you! I don't want you here! Get out! Get out! I'm tired of accepting you all the time . . . I hate you. Leave!

*IT ISN'T UP TO YOU, LAURA PALMER.
YOU SHOULD WATCH THAT EGO. QUITE
UNBELIEVABLE.*

Fuck you.

*CRYING ISN'T GOING TO STOP ME FROM
STAYING EITHER. I'M IMMUNE TO YOUR
EMOTIONAL, ADOLESCENT, FUCKING,
LESBIAN WHORE WHINING AND SELF-
PITY. I'M THE BEST THING IN YOUR LIFE.*

You aren't. It's not true!

ISN'T IT?

Stop lying to me. I have better things in my life
than you. I know it.

OH, YES? NAME ONE.

My parents.

*DOUBT IT. THEY HAVEN'T KEPT ME
FROM GETTING TO YOU, HAVE THEY?
NEITHER ONE TALKS TO YOU THE WAY
THEY USED TO. THEY STOPPED CARING A
LONG TIME AGO. THEY PUT UP WITH YOU.
NOTHING MORE. I'M BETTER.*

Donna.

*THE 'BEST FRIEND' YOU NEVER SPEAK
TO? THE ONE YOU LEFT BEHIND IN EX-*

CHANGE FOR DRUGS? YOU ARE SADLY MIS-
TAKEN.

I have myself. Me. I'm better than you are!

NO. I HAVE YOU. YOU BELONG TO ME.
YOU DON'T DO ANYTHING I DON'T ALLOW
YOU TO DO. I RUN YOUR LIFE, AND I STEER
YOU AS I WISH.

No!

STILL HERE.

You are not real! I refuse to believe that you are
real! I am only imagining you . . . I make you . . . I'll
just stop! You'll have to leave if I stop believing!

TRY AGAIN. I'VE BEEN HERE FOR YEARS
AND YEARS. YOUR BELIEF DOESN'T MEAN
A THING. YOUR OPINION IS NOTHING.
THINK ABOUT IT. LOOK AT YOUR LIFE.
YOU GO FUCKING AROUND WITH PEOPLE.
DRUGS ALL THE TIME. YOU'LL BE SIXTEEN
SOON. YOUR LIFE IS SHIT AND YOU'RE NOT
EVEN SIXTEEN YET. LOOK IN THE MIRROR
AND SEE FOR YOURSELF. YOU ARE
NOTHING.

What . . . do you want?

I WANT YOU.

Why? What for!

ENTERTAINMENT. I ENJOY WATCHING YOU FIGHT THE TRUTH.

What fucking truth?

YOUR LIFE IS WORTHLESS TO EVERY- ONE, INCLUDING YOURSELF. I DO YOU A GREAT FAVOR. I TEACH YOU. YOU OWE ME YOUR LOYALTY. YOU OWE ME EVERY- THING.

I owe you nothing.

'I'M THE BEST THING IN YOUR LIFE.

Goodbye!

I'LL BE HERE.

Fuck you.

SOON. YOU WILL.

Stop.

SEE YOU IN THE DARK ... LAURA PALMER.

Fuck you! Fuck you! Fuck you! Fuck you!
Stay the fuck away from me this time. You're in my head. No one else sees you or hears you, so you must be in my head. I'm not letting you back into this room. Never. You are only an idea. You are a fear. You are only my little-girl, fear-of-the-woods creation!

See! Can't come back now, can you!

You have no power if I don't give it to you . . . This time I'll keep you away. This is my life! It's mine! You have no place here . . . Ha!

I have work to do. Sleep to get. You are dead. You aren't even a memory.

Laura

P.S. *WATCH THE WINDOW, LAURA PALMER.*

Dear Diary,   December 15, 1987

I am sorry I have not written in so long, but I've been working so hard! There is so much you don't know!

First of all, I decided to make a deal with the Hornes. I realized, when I was up there last, that Johnny seemed lifeless, unattended to. Sad. So I proposed to them that I would tutor Johnny, three times a week, spend at least an hour, hour and a half with him, reading, talking, etc., for a small amount of cash weekly. They loved the idea, and have agreed to pay me cash, $50 a week, $200 a month.

The money helps me a lot with the coke, but it's mostly nice to be around Johnny because he loves me no matter what I do when I'm not around him. He doesn't hurt me or tease me or want to sleep with me or tie me up or cut me or any of the millions of things I feel like people do to me all the time ... Always touching me and taking something, always wanting more, and more and more.

All Johnny wants is for me to read to him. *Sleeping Beauty* is his favorite. He likes to rest his head in my lap and look up at me as I read to him. We take a moment every so often to look at the pictures, and I will sometimes have to explain the pictures, as well as some parts of the story, in a way that Johnny will better understand them. He often gets this very confused, lost look on his face, as if he is afraid he doesn't understand anything. I always stop when I see him feeling that way and go over it with him.

Many afternoons we go out on to the front lawn and play with his bow and arrow. He has these rubber buffalo that he shoots down from across the yard. He smiles so beautifully when he hits them. It's his high. It is the strangest scene. Johnny out on the lawn, the grass a blinding green under his moccasins, his arrow tight in the bow as he pulls back, smiling. He releases it after several minutes of concentration. The arrow seems to move at a slower than possible pace, Johnny lowers his arms, rises on to his tiptoes, and waits ... Direct hit. He's in the air, jumping, jumping. Then turns to me and smiles this smile of such excitement.

'Indian!' he exclaims.

I congratulate him on a fine shot, and encourage several more. He is always pleased to do so. I have to do a lot of lines around Johnny, or rather, in the bathroom ... as often as needed.

It is horrible when I lose patience with him. It happened once and I felt miserable until I was certain he had either forgotten the incident or had forgiven me.

I will not go into the details, because my behavior was too horrible. To put it simply, I did a convincing as hell imitation of BOB. It was cruel. The ugliest I had ever felt. I made sure to apologize and explain as best I could as soon as it happened. I wanted him to know I realized it and stopped.

I went and scraped up enough out of the bullet and a couple of vials at the bottom of my purse, to get high. I could think. It's only hard when I don't have it. That's why Bobby and I are seeing each other so innocently and so frequently. But you don't know about all that, do you? Well, hang on.

I have to open up the bedpost here ... and do a couple of lines before Mom comes up to tell me I've got dishes, garbage, etc., to take care of. Shit. I can't believe how different my life is when I simply walk out the front door of this house.

I'll be back as soon as I can.

Laura

Dear Diary,   December 16, 1987

I'm sorry that it is a whole day later, but Mom and I
had a talk in the kitchen while I did the dishes, and it
lasted almost four hours. Dad came home and joined
us for about forty-five minutes before heading up to
bed early.

I guess Benjamin has him working pretty hard on
some new plan. Dad just rolls his eyes when Mom and
I ask how it's going.

Sometimes I think that my mom and I could be the
best of friends. Every once in a while I will look into
her eyes and think, I wonder if Mom has ever felt
anything that I'm feeling? I sense that some of my
experiences are ones that she would understand, but
she comes from a family and a generation that doesn't
really like to talk about things that make them uncomfortable.

Maybe BOB makes her feel uncomfortable. Maybe
Dad knows BOB too, but Mom won't let us talk abut
him because it makes everyone . . . so upset . . . I don't
know.

I guess we had a good talk anyway, because I know
she was very happy when she went up to bed. I stayed
downstairs for a while, then walked outside and studied
the wall BOB always climbs to get to my window. It's
amazing he hasn't killed himself or at least fallen.

The nights I've snuck out, I've always had help
getting down. I wonder if I could make it so that he
would fall? He'd find a way up no matter what, and I
still want Bobby Briggs to deliver my blow through
that window . . . have a quickie while my parents are
asleep or out.

That's what I wanted to get back to. Bobby Briggs.

We are seeing each other like guys and girls do when they're in high school. It's weird. I see Donna more now, and she's with Mike. I guess she's happy, but the two of them remind me of a chewing-gum commercial or something. 'Happiness and ambition, athletics and academics, rah, rah, rah.'

Last week I went through an entire bullet of coke just trying to deal with having a burger with them after the movies. Bobby and I didn't eat. Bobby had eaten a ton of junk in the theater, and I was too high to even look at food. Donna stuffed her face, and I knew she'd pay for that in zits and in the seams of her clothes when she got up the next day. I'll bet she gained five pounds. Mike is a pig. He just kept shoving fries and hamburgers into his mouth, like swallowing wasn't necessary or something. I swear!

I don't like the way he looks at Donna either. I worry about her, because he seems like such an asshole . . . thinking he's something of a superhero wth his letter jacket on all the time. Shit. I don't care. Donna's smart. I just can't believe Dr Hayward hasn't said something.

So, the reason I'm seeing Bobby this way, going to the movies, dinner, studying at his house, going out to the gazebo and necking, taking his father's car to the Pearl Lakes, etc., is because he finally agreed to start selling cocaine for Leo. For me. I had been waiting for him to say he would, but he wanted me to promise I'd act like his girl again. So I do. When I want to, or when I'm out of blow. I really like Bobby, but he could never understand what happens to me sometimes.

The whole reason I go out for the orgies at Leo's, the reason I let him tie me up and hit me sometimes, the whole reason, besides a strange enjoyment, is because I feel like I belong in dark places like that. I belong with sleazy men who are actually crying babies. I tease them and pretty soon they're calling me 'Mommy' and burying their heads in my lap crying about their pain . . . and then I have to tell them what to do. They like it that way. I belong with them. I must, or I wouldn't be so good at it.

I'll tell them what to do to me. Order them to do it. And when they do, when it's feeling nice and I can tell that they are really trying, I start telling them what I'm feeling. How wonderful they are. How they are 'good, good boys. Such good boys.' I tell them that Mommy is happy. They love it. A child and a man all at once.

All of them, these friends of Leo's and Jacques's (who I must tell you about!), are very nice to me. If I ever needed help, I believe that they would be there for me. I don't know. I've been wrong before.

So Bobby sells the coke around town, and Leo sells his usual stuff to people across the border, over in Canada. I always get at least an eight-ball free, and then each time I see Leo, he fills my bullet or a vial if I can find one.

Bobby makes really good money and everybody's happy. That's the whole point of life, right? The only thing that pisses me off is that the other day, when I went with Bobby to get the drug money from my safety-deposit box (I wasn't going to hide thousands of dollars in my bedpost!), he said that Mike was going to start helping him sell.

I threw a fit and told him that if he did – and Mike ever told Donna – I would never, ever speak to him again. Donna would tell her father. I know it. I wouldn't be able to handle that. Dr Hayward being disappointed in me . . . that would kill me for sure.

Bobby said he wasn't sure about it yet. But I made him promise anyway, and he did.

After that, we went out to the tree where the empty football is buried, near Leo's house. The money and drugs are exchanged through the buried football. Leo always makes fun of Bobby for his choice of hiding places. 'The football hero' he calls him. Bobby is a football hero, though. At least the school thinks he is.

Jacques said that he used to play football, until he found out that you didn't have to ram yourself into a herd of huge guys all day to make good money. Jacques lives deep in the woods in a cabin with his bird, Waldo. Waldo talks and has learned my name perfectly. Jacques, Jacques Renault, works across the border at a casino somewhere. He's a big, fat guy, but he can really turn me on sometimes. He's the little-baby/big-man type, too, except that he knows a lot more about a woman's body than even Leo.

I went out to Jacques's by myself one night, and we got super high and played all sorts of amazing sex games with each other. It got to the point that all he had to say was 'Show me, little girl . . . show me,' and I was reeling!

Waldo repeated almost everything we said all night and into the early morning. The whole way home I kept hearing Waldo say, 'Show me . . . Show me . . . Little girl . . . Little girl.' That was the morning I realized that the orgies with Leo took place in front of Jacques's cabin. There was the chair . . . I sat in it for a minute, and knew.

I'll write again soon. I have plans for the night.

L

Dear Diary,   December 21, 1987

    Christmas is almost here. I'm starting to look for another job, something with a real paycheck every two weeks ... real money. Mom is beginning to worry about how little I'm eating lately. I love it. I swear I've never liked my body before. I still have nice breasts, and curved hips, but no fat there like before. None of the guys I've been with have said anything but great stuff about my body.

    I need a job in order to have more money, and also to be able to tell Mom that I ate while I was at work. I can't force another dinner down my throat like I've been doing.

    Leo and Jacques gave me a few issues of *Fleshworld Magazine* the other night. I opened the pages and did some of the poses for them, did some dancing, a few things for myself ... and let them watch me until all three of us came together.

    I know it sounds dirty, but I am only doing what I am suddenly used to doing ... Creating a show for other people to look at, while inside my head I go into a dream. A whole audience, at least a hundred people. (I do that because the more people there are, the more it seems like it is okay, and not a hidden or bad thing.) All of the people, men and women, watch me. They watch how I move, how little sounds come out of my mouth when I begin to feel warm inside ... I dream of a man or woman, sometimes both ... and how I see them in the front row, the quietest of all. Let's say it is a man for description's sake.

    So I come down to the level of the audience, and I'm wearing something black and see-through, and I take him by the hand and make him come on to the stage with me. He doesn't want to, but I promise him I won't embarrass or hurt him. He believes me and we go up into the lights.

I tell everyone in whispers that this man is beautiful to me, and I tell them why. I describe him so that he becomes confident and aroused all at once. The audience loves him now, just like I do. I usually change the dream each time, but it always ends up with me and my chosen partner making love in front of everyone. I get a high sometimes when I think that BOB will see me in this dream and realize he should finally set me free.

So I have these magazines, and people send their fantasies in sometimes and they get printed. I told Leo and Jacques the night they gave them to me, and we played around, about some of the fantasies I have sometimes. Both of them said that I should send one of them in, maybe more than one, and see if I can get one printed. They said that if I do, they will create the printed fantasy just the way I write it. Just the way I want it.

I think I will. I like the idea of a special night, planned ahead of time, all for Laura Palmer.

Maybe I'll write the fantasy in here, too, so that you will know exactly what will be planned if it gets printed. I'll think abut it.

Some of the pictures in the magazines are so . . . dirty. Almost too dirty for me, but I see why some people get turned on by them. They are mostly pictures about people being some place, or with someone who is totally a fantasy person. There is no tomorrow or yesterday. No hours or minutes or rules or parents or mornings or anything to worry about. I like that part, but some of the photos are of women being captured and taken away by these men. I don't really like those too much, because for some reason . . . I don't know what, they remind me too much of BOB's visits. The women are too young or innocent or something.

I like being taken by someone, but I like being teased and given little dreams and ideas. I don't like fears or lies or yelling, and that is what some of these pictures are like. Darkness in sex is okay, as long as it is strange, mysterious darkness, and not the darkness of hell or nightmares or dying.

That stuff isn't for me. I like the good stuff. Almost really bad, but just teasing with the bad, not taking its hand and pulling it inside.

I have to go shopping for Christmas presents tomorrow. God, I have no idea what to get anyone. I suppose it's bad for me to wish for coke for Christmas . . . A ton of white, fluffy snow all over me.

More later, Laura

Dear Diary,   December 23, 1987

Remember the night that Leo and Bobby and I went out to Low Town to buy coke? Remember? I stole the kilo and everything went crazy and we had to make a run for it because everyone started firing their guns? I just had a dream about it.

I never even really thought about the fact that Bobby probably killed that guy when he shot him. Bobby actually shot him, and I watched and didn't care! I think I just told myself that I was dreaming or something, but I know that's a lie, completely.

I just called Bobby at home and talked to him about it for a minute. At first, he was okay, and we were trying to whisper and talk about it at the same time so that no one would hear . . . and he started to cry, I think. I couldn't really tell for sure, but I think maybe he had lied to himself the way I did. I don't think either of us realized what we'd done.

I was on the phone in my room, and I just stared at the bedpost while Bobby was silent on the other end of the line. I think I am in over my head with the coke, but I just can't stop. It has been the only thing besides Johnny Horne and all sorts of sex that has kept me going . . . I wonder if the dream I had means I'm going to hell. Me and Bobby Briggs in hell, side by side, doing coke with the devil. I know that isn't funny. It isn't funny at all.

In the dream, the guy Bobby shot stood up after the bullet went into his chest, and he said that death had given him sixty seconds to tell us our future.

He said, 'You, with the gun . . . watch yourself. Those who die this way memorize the face of their killer, and tell Death about the face. Death comes looking for you. Takes your friends, or a parent. Death takes what you have allowed it to. Murder is just a way of shaking Death's hand and telling him, "What is mine is yours."'

In the dream, Bobby looked at me and back to the guy he shot. The guy said, 'You watch that girlfriend of yours. Someone down here is saving her a seat.'

And it was over.

I told Bobby about the dream, and he said he had to go. He didn't say where, he just said he had to get off the phone and go.

I bought Bobby a pair of his favorite boots for Christmas. They were expensive, but I had saved a lot, believe it or not, from my sessions with Johnny. I guess I started to feel like it was bad to use that money for coke. I haven't needed it lately because Jacques and Leo have been into getting me high and playing games.

I don't even have to call them any more. Jacques calls me, and if Mom or Dad answers, he says he's calling back about a job I applied for. I always know it's going to be a wild night when Mom says that the phone is for me ... 'Some gentleman calling about your application . . .?'

I should get a real job. Somewhere that I can dress up a little and be high and pretty and paid.

Diary, I hope that my dream was just a nightmare memory, and that if the man in Low Town is dead, that he is somewhere nice, or that at least there is no pain for him. I'm afraid that if he had pain now, that somehow Death would save a seat for me. Death would probably let BOB hold that seat. I don't want to think that.

I'm going to take a shower and do some blasts. I

need to finish Donna's Christmas present. Did I tell you about it? No, I guess not . . . I don't see it above. Well, I was feeling like I should do something a good friend would do, and I wanted to give her something that would take her mind off all the ideas she has about how much trouble I might be in. That's my business now.

I called Dr Hayward, talked for a while, and had him sneak Donna's blue-jean jacket to me when she wasn't home. I went to the crafts shop in town and bought all the beads, patches, and embroidery-thread colors she likes. I have been up for the past few nights sewing everything on to the jacket in neat designs. I know she has wanted to do it herself for ages, so I hope she likes this. I need her to stop worrying. It only causes trouble.

See you later, Diary.

Love, Laura

Dear Diary,   December 23, 1987

I finished Donna's jacket, and it is now 4:20 a.m. I
can't get to sleep and I'm thinking about going to
Jacques's or Leo's to look for some pot, or maybe
Jacques has one of those Valiums he gave me a couple
of weeks ago. That was great. Maybe I'll call first. I
don't want to walk through the woods without a good
reason.

                                    Be back in a minute, L

Back again, and so glad I didn't walk all the way out
there without calling. I'm not sure if I told you about
the night I got lost, and so afraid in the darkness of the
woods, that I just sat down and cried until the sky got
light enough to find my way home. I was offered a
ride home, but I was afraid that Dad would be home
late, and I would pull up with Leo or Jacques right
when he got to the house. He likes his little girl the
way she used to be . . . maybe still should be . . . No.

Anyway, I talked to Leo first, and he said he missed
me. Shelley was back from her aunt's funeral, and the
inheritance he thought she was getting never came.
She might have to go back in about a week because her
aunt left her a lot of the stuff.

He asked if I had sent in my fantasy. I told him I
was thinking of working on it, but I needed to come
down a little. He laughed a little and said that Jacques
had something to tell me.

Jacques came on the line and I told him I was sorry
to call so late. He said he'd only be mad if I hadn't
called, then he called me his 'sweet baby' and I smiled,
but didn't say anything.

He said Leo told him why I had called, but that he was already prepared for this to happen. He told me that in the bra I was wearing the other night, the white lace one, he had hidden one of my Christmas presents.

I asked him to hold on so I could get it, but he said Leo needed the phone.

Shelley was waiting for him to call from some truck stop somewhere out of state. I guess he doesn't want to be around her right now. I hung up and searched through my drawer for the bra.

The white lace one is one of Jacques's favorites. It has a wire support and it makes my breasts look really nice. So I found the bra . . . thank God I hadn't had time to do my hand-washing!

Inside the fabric cup, I felt a package, about the size of a cigarette pack, but thinner. I'm so lucky Mom didn't find this. When I opened it, I realized that the wrapper was a folded, torn-out page from *Fleshworld*, showing a guy built kind of like Jacques, kneeling in front of a really pretty blonde girl. I think she was the prettiest girl I'd ever seen in that magazine. In the photo, this girl was almost naked with a parrot on her shoulder, and the man was kissing her feet like he adored her. At the bottom of the page, Jacques had written, 'Thinking of you, fantasy girl.'

Inside there were four Valium, two joints, a quarter gram of coke, and a silver wand. Brand-new and shiny. I became so excited, I almost forgot what time it was, and I heard Mom call my name to see if I was okay.

I flipped all but one of the lights off in my room shoved the packet back into the bra, and slipped it under the bed. I put Donna's jacket across my lap and pretended that I had fallen asleep.

A moment later Mom came in, woke me gently, and

told me to hop in bed. I was brilliant in the role of innocent, sleeping daughter. I kissed her and mumbled a little, and after she left, I waited almost forty minutes before leaving the bed. I brought all of the treats up on to the comforter and played in the dark, until it was safe to put a towel under the door and switch the light back on. I only used the night-light, because it was sexier than the bright one over my head.

I went into a deep, drugged, happy, thoughtful, nasty, and still-innocent fantasy. I'll have to tell more later . . . I feel so dreamy right now . . . I'm on two Valium, another line of coke, and half a joint. I splurged, but damn if I don't feel absolutely perfect.

I think I'll look at *Fleshworld* issues for a while before it gets light out. I'll either tell you the fantasy I just had, or one I get a new idea for from the magazines.

Night, night. L

Dear Diary,   Christmas Eve Day, 1987

I'm at the gazebo, trying to get the tunes of Christmas carols out of my head. Mom has been playing them all morning. I like Christmas, but with my head feeling like it was, I could hardly stand any more of it. Dad caught me when I was leaving and asked for a dance with his favorite little girl. Dad and I hadn't danced in years, I don't think.

Memories of parties at the Great Northern, with the blur of streamers and buffets and crystal came into my head, the way I saw them as Dad and I turned round and round. He would spin me fast enough to make my stomach flip in the right way, and we would laugh and laugh.

This dance this morning was in the living room. The lights on the tree were already turned on so that Mom could bake in the true spirit of the season, and I watched the red and green and blue and white pass by me. I looked into Dad's eyes so that I wouldn't get too dizzy, and I saw his eyes light up, and a tear form, and then drop slowly down his cheek. The spinning slowed, and he grabbed me tight, held me as if he were afraid of something.

Mom came out of the kitchen and said that seeing Dad and me hugging in front of the Christmas tree was the best present she could ask for.

So many strange things happen in life. My life, I mean. Just hours before the dancing, I was in my room buried deep in a very, very different world. I hope I never have to choose between the two. Each one makes me happy for different reasons.

I came out here to write my fantasy out, but it is

almost too cold and too pretty for me to think about it now. Here and now, at least.

I'm gonna head over to the Double R and get some hot coffee. Maybe I'll find a private booth.

Back soon. L

Dear Diary,   Christmas Eve Day, 1987, later

When I walked in here, the Double R Diner, Norma immediately poured me a cup of coffee. Perfect. I told her I wanted to do some private writing, some stuff for school, so I was going to the booth in back instead of the counter.

Before taking my seat, I picked up my cup of coffee from the counter and noticed a very elderly woman sitting very quietly about two seats down. Her face was buried in a book bearing the name *Shroud of Innocence*. She turned the page, absorbed in the story completely. I saw by her plate that she had eaten a piece of cherry pie à la mode and was on her way to quite a caffeine rush.

I looked at Norma, who smiled, and I shook my head, like, what a great character. A nice, kind-faced old woman, out at the diner for pie and coffee over a good book. I went to the back booth and got comfortable. I was about to get into the fantasy with you, but . . . Shelley Johnson came out of the back room.

Leo's wife is prettier than I had remembered. I watched her. I was very careful to study her body when she moved, her smile, her voice. I was suddenly going back and forth between feeling totally competitive to feeling like I had no chance at all over her. Then I heard her saying something about Leo to Norma. Something about how he's never home, and when he is, he just wants to get it on. I had won. I felt like a bitch for thinking it, but I thought, I've been doing it with him for quite some time now . . . I'll keep doing it if you won't.

I knew that wasn't what she meant, but I couldn't feel sorry for her, or I would never be able to see Leo again. I couldn't deal with that.

I watched as the old woman from the counter tried to make her way out of the diner. It was obvious that it was difficult for her, and I felt for a minute like I should get up and help her . . . but Shelley did it.

Norma came over with more coffee and said that the old woman comes in a lot, but it is difficult for her to move. Her walker helps, but she is constantly struggling with each step, as I could probably see.

Norma said that there are a lot of senior citizens in Twin Peaks who have no one to take care of them. There is no place for them to go . . . at least not without heading into Montana. Most want to stay here. It's quiet. They're happy for the most part.

I started tossing this around in my head. A problem to solve. I would do more than just help the woman to the door! Uh-oh. Competitive Laura, front and center. I hadn't felt like this since elementary school. I was fired up about finding a way to help the senior citizens Norma mentioned.

I left a note for Norma when I paid the check. I said that I wanted to talk more about helping these people. I told her she could call me when she got a chance.

I'm going to try to catch a ride to Johnny's with Ed Hurley. I can see him outside the window. I hope he's going that way.

Speak soon, Laura

P.S. It is late on Christmas Eve night. I'll say more later, but I heard about Norma's 'upsetting phone call' earlier at the diner.

When I was with Johnny, I heard Benjamin talking to the sheriff or something. I got the whole story after that, because Benjamin was upset about it.

I know Norma won't be able to call me back right away because Hank, her husband, who I've never been really impressed with, killed a man on the highway late last night, coming back on the Lucky 21 from the border, I think.

Anyway, he's going to do time now for vehicular manslaughter. I'm glad he'll be away for a while. Norma always seems so upset by him. I'm sorry for Norma. Not for Hank.

Dear Diary,   January 3, 1988

Christmas was interesting. Dad took three days off and made it incredibly difficult, without realizing it, for me to get high. I had to fake premenstrual cramps so that he would let me leave and go to my room to be alone.

As I went up the stairs, I stopped because I heard Dad say, 'But it's the new year ... I'm on holiday ... Why does she want to be alone?'

I could hear my mother explaining, in that kind, so very wise voice, that I was a teenager. 'Parents are like the plague to teenagers, Leland ... We're lucky she's even spent this much time with us. She was only out for three hours on New Year's Eve, and she was back before midnight to celebrate with us.'

Mom was doing a great job, so I proceeded upstairs to my room for some privacy and a well-deserved line.

A line heals all wounds.

Bobby and I actually had a really good New Year's Eve, like Mom said, for three hours. Eight-thirty to eleven-thirty. We went out to the golf course, where about thirty other couples had the same plan: grab a blanket, and the drug of your choice (alcohol came out the winner, though Bobby and I smoked a joint), and curl up on the grass and watch the stars.

We were away from the others, but close enough so that as we were smoking our joint, we could overhear the other couples making New Year's resolutions, and New Year's wishes on the stars above us.

Bobby turned on to his side and put the joint in my mouth. I took a hit, and I remember thinking, 'He's going to say something serious here ... I can feel it.' He took a quick hit and held it in, looked upward, exhaled ... looked back at me.

'Laura?'

'Yeah, Bobby.' I was feeling warm and good. I love pot.

'Laura, I'm sorry things are the way they are sometimes . . . between us. I mean, I wish we were both, I don't know.'

'Bobby, c'mon. I was listening to you. Go on.'

'I can't speak for you, but I feel like sometimes you and I are so close. Even when we aren't sleeping together. We're just close . . .'

I turned on to my side and leaned my head on my hand. We hadn't talked in ages. We were even stoned, too. 'Go ahead. I agree.'

'Other times – I don't know what the hell is what. It's like I'm doing all my life stuff . . . all of Bobby Briggs's stuff . . . but it doesn't affect me like maybe it should. You know?'

I wanted to understand, so I gave it a shot. 'You mean like, there's a part of you who goes to school, does chores, goes to work part-time, or whatever, but the other part, the part that feels things and cares about things, is inside somewhere asleep?'

'Yeah . . . yeah, you sorta got it. But I'm skipping my whole point here.'

He offered me the last hit off the joint. I decided to take it and hit off it while he held it in his fingertips. I love the way Bobby's skin smells. I took the last hit, and he went on.

'I was thinking that you and I are together just because it was where we expected we'd be. Is this making sense?'

I nodded. I knew what he was saying.

'I just don't want us to be together because of a deal we made because of the . . . I mean, Leo and all the "snow" around his place. Sometimes I don't think that matters, and other times, I think that if you had to choose between the snow and me . . . Well, I think I'd lose.'

I looked down at the blanket we were on. I tried to see its pattern in the darkness, but saw only the vague shadows of the black-and-red plaid I knew it was. I picked at the wool nervously. Finally I was able to look up at him.

I told him that sometimes I would choose the coke over him, but that *I would sometimes choose coke over anyone*. I told him I didn't want to hurt him, or anyone else. I just feel that sometimes I am better company to only myself, because of what is happening in my life, than I am or would be to anyone else.

He told me that he could understand that, maybe, but he wanted to know if I thought the coke was the problem.

I told him, very quietly, that I started really liking coke because I didn't have to think about 'the problem'. I told him I liked pot for the same reason.

I remember saying, 'I can't tell you anything, Bobby. I just can't. I understand if you want to leave me because of it, but I just can't tell you or anyone.' I knew that the coke was a problem, but it was nothing next to BOB.

He didn't say anything for the longest time. Then, he kissed me. He kissed me for a long time, and when he stopped, and looked at me, he said I didn't know all of his problems either, and that he would try and understand the times I didn't want to jump up and down with joy. Something like that. Then he said that he felt we belonged together, at least right now he felt that.

Things were strange for the rest of the night. Not bad strange, just different from the way Bobby and I usually were together. We made out for hours, and then, and I say this with all honesty, *we made love*.

No games, no control, no ego, no bad thoughts or thoughts about anything except what was happening. It was amazing. Both of us agreed.

I knew I loved Bobby at that moment, and I know I love him now. I just wonder if I can let myself feel any of these wonderful, pure feelings without getting myself in trouble with BOB.

Why do I always, always have to second-guess my life and my feelings? Why can't I just love him, fight with him, kiss him, etc., without worrying that I'll die because of it?

Why do other girls get to have happy lives? Why can't I just tell him the truth?

YOU DON'T KNOW THE TRUTH.

You're here.

SMART GIRL.

What do you want?

JUST CHECKING IN.

Fine. I'm here. You checked in. Now go.

I SAW YOUR LIGHT ON SIX NIGHTS IN A ROW.

So did anyone who walked down the street.

LAURA PALMER . . . BE NICE.

You never taught me that.

NICE. DEFINITION: DON'T BE RUDE.

I'm to the point where I don't care any more, BOB. Do whatever you need to do.

I DON'T NEED ANYTHING.

How nice for you. Now get out of my head!

I WANT THINGS.

I can't hear you.

WE BOTH KNOW YOU CAN.

Diary, I am here in my room alone. I have had a very nice day, and now I am sitting in bed, on top of the covers, writing to you. I know that I can control this. I know I can *SEE BOB BECAUSE HE IS REAL. A REAL THREAT. TO YOU, LAURA PALMER. TO EVERYONE AROUND YOU. BE NICE. BE GLAD TO SEE ME.*

Never!

YOU ONLY MAKE THINGS WORSE THIS WAY.

That's impossible! Get the fuck out of my head!

I LIKE IT HERE. MIGHT STAY AWHILE.

Fine.

BE NICE.

Nice? Gee, BOB, is that you? How wonderful of you to drop into my head. The door is always open, you know. Why don't you and I go for a walk in the woods, BOB? C'mon. Let's take a walk. You can pick the day's game. What will it be . . . sex?

NO. YOU'RE DIRTY.

You are wrong.

TRY AGAIN, LAURA PALMER.

You aren't worth it.

I HAVE A MESSAGE.

A message from . . .?

A DEAD MAN.

I'm insane! You are not real! It's simple. I need to get to a doctor because I am creating this. I am in charge. Calm down. I have to calm down.

MESSAGE: A SEAT IS BEING SAVED FOR YOU . . . LAURA PALMER.

Stop!

BACK SOON.

See? You are in my head. No one besides you knew the details of my dream of death. Not even Bobby.
BOB is not real.

Laura

IN THE EYES OF THE VISITOR

I am something constant
An animal of prey
No matter how many times
I am attacked
Sent home to the nest
Bleeding

I stay.

I am the greatest of fools.
A defect in the cycle of life.
No creature with any
Respect
For life
For itself
For its enemy
Stands again and again
In the enemy's path.

I stay.

I have no respect
Left
For the enemy
For the nest
For the tree
For the prey.
I wait
Without choice
I challenge his threat
To take this baby
And hand it to Death.

I have some good news.

I spent the afternoon with Johnny today. He was in especially good spirits and I decided that the day was too crisp and beautiful for either of us to stay inside.

Out to the front lawn we went. The lawn is a great expanse of green grass and flowers tended year-round by a staff of men and women with green thumbs, fingers, and the rest. It is the perfect place to spend a Saturday afternoon. I usually see Johnny on Mondays, Wednesdays, and Fridays, but apparently a specialist came to see him yesterday, and Benjamin asked if I would mind coming today instead.

Between you and me, Diary, today was much better for me. *Yesterday*, for the second time ever, I ditched school. I spent the whole day going through my bedroom, reorganizing things. Mom and Dad were gone all day until six p.m. at some convention.

I rearranged my furniture a bit and bought a lock for my bedroom door. It was easy to install because it was only a chain lock. A few screws later and I had privacy. If only everything were that simple. I didn't ask Mom or Dad if the idea bothered them, so I chose the chain, figuring they will think I only want the room locked when I am there. This is not the case, but for now, until I can think of a reason that the two of them would approve of, and not question . . . *this is it*.

I went through some of the more recent *Fleshworld Magazines* and found that this is the time to submit a fantasy of mine. There is a contest going on for one month only, 'Fantasy of the Month'. The winner receives $200. Anonymity is allowed, although a mailing address is necessary. My safety-deposit box allows me six weeks' free use of a PO box. I'll get over there later today and take care of it, I guess No harm in entering as long as I use a different name.

Today, I needed a fresh start. My time with Johnny was wonderful, and dare I say, almost spiritual. We were lying face to face on our stomachs while he requested that I tell him story after story.

The moment I would finish one, he would applaud and say, 'Story!'

He didn't want to be read to. He wanted non-fiction. Life experiences. All that went through my head at first was, *this is impossible*. I can't tell him any of my stories! But eventually I realized that not only did I have some suitable stories, but that I was being far too forgetful of Johnny's mental level. I could have recited the grocery list, with intonations like those of storytelling, and he would have stood up to cheer. He wanted to feel included in a face-to-face discussion, some interaction. Spoken to rather than spoken about.

I was able to stop pitying myself and to recall some of the happiest times in my life, as well as some of the most sad. Each story helped me as much as it did Johnny. I had a chance to realize how far away I had kept happiness, and how much I missed it.

As you can imagine, I basically took full advantage of the chance to just babble on to someone, story or no story, uninterrupted. No questions, no comments, no judgments on who I was or where I'd be going, once dead. Johnny is simply the best listener around.

I felt very refreshed and even entertained, thanks to Johnny's innocent mimicry of faces in conversation. He was always nodding as if he understood . . . smiling when I would, and at the mention of the words 'the end', he would put all his energy into applauding me.

At about two-thirty, Mrs Horne, who I was surprised to see without shopping bags under each arm, and a plane ticket in her mouth, called the two of us in for lunch. When I looked at my watch, I was shocked to see that almost three and a half hours had gone by.

Before I could get up, Johnny took hold of my hands and smiled one of his biggest smiles ever. He closed his eyes, reopened them and said his very first sentence! *He said, 'I love you, Laura.'*

I could go on and on about how wonderful that was, as an incredible leap for him, as well as for me. It was the highest compliment I have ever been given.

After lunch I left to open my PO box. I'm going to have to think carefully about this fantasy. Perhaps I shouldn't write it here, in your pages, because unless it is printed, it didn't really happen to me. Did it?

More soon, Laura

I've been going over and over my sexual experiences and have decided that it is important to look at at least the initials of each person I have been with.

B.
B.B.
L.J.
R.P.
J.C.L.
T.T.R.
D.M.J.
C.D.M.
M.R.M.
D.G.
G.N.
G.P.
D.L.
M.R.
M.F.
R.D.
T.T.O.
K.M.Y.
S.R.
A.N.
M.D.
J.H.
M.F.
C.S.
B.G.D.
L.D.
J.H. And several unseen unknowns – out by the cabin.
T.P.S.

M.T.
G.L.
J.S.
M.V.L.
C.S.
D.M.J.
A.W.N.
M.S.R.
D.D.
S.C.
H.P.
B.E.

Dear Diary,   February 9, 1988

Something very strange has happened.

I snuck out of the house last night to go see Leo and Jacques at the cabin. Ronnette was supposed to be there too, and I was pretty excited about seeing her. Besides, it had been ages since I could talk about things with a girl. Donna just wouldn't understand all of this. I needed girl talk, badly.

I began walking, but then decided I was too impatient (a big mistake), and so I headed toward Highway 21 in hopes of hitching a ride the next mile or two to the cabin.

About fifteen minutes passed before I saw a big rig, just like Leo's, coming down the road. I stuck my thumbs out, and sure enough, the truck pulled over and the door opened. Inside the cab were four very drunk, very drugged-up truckers who, from what I could understand, had been in town drinking. One of them offered me a beer, and I took it. Not really because I wanted it, but because I was suddenly afraid of upsetting any of them.

I told them where I needed to be dropped off, and just before my stop, I finished the beer and began peeling the label off the bottle nervously. *I realized we were not going to stop.*

I told the driver he was about to pass my 'dropping point', and he told me I should know better than to be hitchhiking late at night with a body like mine, poured into my jeans and T-shirt the way it was.

I swear I was not 'poured' into my clothes, Diary. My only mistake was leaving the trail through the woods and heading out to the highway alone. It was a big mistake, but I . . . I wasn't thinking.

We drove up through the Twin Peaks to a seedy little motel that I wasn't even convinced was owned and open, due to its shabby appearance. But, needless to say, these guys already had two rooms and basically carried me into the first. I caught the room number, 207. In case I could call for help, I would know where I was. I wasn't sure I'd get out of here in one piece.

All of them became incredibly rowdy. They were screaming at the top of their lungs and shouting out vulgar language. I thought for a moment that if I could just stand up without anyone's noticing, I could outrun any of these drunk jerk-offs. I was as careful as I could be, but the moment I tried to stand, three of the four guys were on me.

'Where are you goin', baby?'

'Hey, why don't you and I go into the next room and do a little private dancing?' He was the ugliest of all of them.

I knew that if I didn't do something soon, something to manipulate the situation my way, they would become violent and most likely rape me. I realized that I might never come out of it alive. *I was horrified.*

I forced a smile. 'Listen . . . all of you.'

One of the guys looked at me like I was out of my mind to be taking such 'liberties'. He was interested, though, in what I was going to say, because he got all of them to shut up and gather around the chair I was in.

I squeezed yet another false smile out of my face and went on, 'Listen, if you all want to play tonight . . . and you know what I mean . . . then let's do it right, okay?'

One of the guys, the one with tattoos everywhere, stepped up to the chair, and kicked the hell out of it.

Five or six times. I tried not to look as mortified as I was. He bent down, greasy hair in his face, his breath like garbage. 'You better watch your mouth, little hitchhiker, 'cause where I'm from, a hole like you would never dare tell a man that he ain't doin' a job that beats all other jobs.'

'I didn't mean to imply that you weren't experienced. I can tell that you are just by watching you move.' God, they were all so awful. My tongue was shaking in my mouth, nervous and lying. I was so stupid!

Another of the guys, the youngest, and the only one with any concern for me at all, suggested they hear what I had to say.

I slid myself back to an upright position in the chair and looked at all of them, carefully. I thought, just go for it. It's either going to work or they're probably going to rape and kill you. You can't let people like this take your life. Just make it up as you go along, Laura.

'Okay, I am not opposed to drinking, drugs, or sex, all in measured doses. I am not opposed to getting a little kinky, getting motherly, or becoming a little girl ... more of a little girl, nor am I opposed to my performing a solo show, for everyone.'

There were belches and nodding heads. Eight big eyes, growing wider.

'I think all of you will like my show *very much* ... I'll even invent some new things for you, new touches ... and if anything should come to you, about what you want to see me do, you come over and whisper in my ear. *I'll play games.*

'But here's the deal: I get a ride back to town, and I walk out of here the same way I walked in. No violence.'

One of the guys decided he was too macho for this and said, 'I'll slap you right upside the head if I get the urge, bitch.'

I gathered my nerves enough to lean toward him and appear confident. 'If you get the urge to slap me, as you said, right upside the head, I haven't done my . . . job.' I swallowed hard. 'You can call me bitch and whatever else, but let's just try and get along . . . okay?'

It took me another forty minutes after they agreed to my show to get them to stop with all of the attitude and the yelling. Finally, I offered each a Valium in his beer and told them to sit on the couch, drink the beer, and I would start.

I have never been so frightened, ever. Forget nightmares, forget near-misses with a speeding car on a wet road, forget BOB even, simply because, in comparison to this, it was four to one. And each of them was big enough to eat my entire body as a snack before lunch.

All of them sat on the couch, except one, who I told to watch the door so that no one would think I was planning an escape. I pulled a chair around to the middle of the room. A wooden chair, nice high back . . . *almost too perfect*. I took a few steps to each side of the room and switched off the lights.

Slowly I began to undress, and each time I removed a piece of clothing, I memorized where I had 'tossed it' so (if they did pass out like I planned) I would be able to dress quickly and get out.

I began to talk to myself. I imagined being stoned so that I could relax. I was so damned afraid that someone was going to jump up and say, 'You're history, baby,' but no one did.

I slowly began the routine of the 'little girl lost in

the woods' . . . a favorite of Leo's and Jacques's because I can become 'Mommy' so fast.

I prayed that I could keep them intrigued long enough to watch their eyelids get heavy. I went to the man at the door, probably the meanest one, and I lifted his hand, which was surprisingly relaxed, on to my chest, and I talked to him softly.

It was a good fifteen minutes that he was touching me and really getting into talking back with me and I could feel him giving in, just like Jacques. One of the others got selfish and said, 'Hey, what about over here!'

'Don't you worry, boys, I don't get tired. I *never* get bored, and it would be impossible to forget who's in this room.' I had to keep all of them happy. I swung the chair around and asked the man with me to kneel down. I told him softly so that it would not appear as a threat, and began to dance. I went all around the room . . . and paid attention to each of them . . . admiring them, anything about them . . . lying . . . (None of them were passing out!)

Finally I made it back to the chair. Next began the hottest part of the whole piece . . . a very rowdy, raunchy sit-and-spin routine during which all of them leaned forward and looked closely at me as I played. I continued this and elaborated on it . . . *extended it*.

I did all I could think of to get them physically and *emotionally* intoxicated. Everyone was looking tired, but they were still managing to clap and whistle.

To be brief, this went on until three of the four guys passed out, and I was left with *one*. A big, round dude with a three-day beard, and saggy eyes. He told me I mesmerized him.

He asked if I wanted to go into the other room. He

said he had the key. I came up close and asked, 'What about the truck? Can we do it there?'

'Sure, it's your back, baby.'

So I grabbed what I could of my clothing, minus the socks and bra, and ventured out into the night, trying to think of a way to get out of this place . . . as soon as possible. I needed to get out. Get high. Get home.

As soon as I was able, I sat in the driver's seat and called him over with my pursed lips. He slid across the vinyl seats fast. He buried himself deep in my chest, and I thought, okay, Laura, find the bottle with your hand . . . there! Don't move too quickly, distract him, and SMASH!

I whacked the guy over the head with the bottle and drew blood. *He was bleeding all over.* I jumped out of the truck and began running, half naked . . . so what! I wanted to get away from them, before they realized what I had done.

I went to Jacques's cabin, hoping he and Leo would be there, still with Ronnette.

When I got there, I was pretty haggard, pretty emotionally beaten. I burst into tears and fell to my knees on the floor. Ronnette came to me and helped get me to the couch. I couldn't stop crying! I was even ashamed that I was able to get myself out of it the way that I did . . . I felt like the dirtiest person ever! BOB was right, he was so right!

I grabbed ahold of Ronnette's arm, and I heard her say, 'There's blood all over her, let's get her cleaned up. She's only going to stay upset with blood all over her body.'

The next thing I remember was waking up in my own bed, with a note clenched in my fist.

Dear Laura –

> *We tried to calm you down as much as possible,
> but you were hysterical . . . and just kept asking to
> go home. I don't think anyone heard us coming in,
> but if you get caught, tell them what happened.*
>   *Everything is okay now. I know you were scared
> . . . Maybe we can see each other in a couple of days
> and talk or something, okay?*

Ronnette

So there's my night. You would think I'd learn, but I guess I just can't for some reason.

I've even had thoughts since waking up this morning about how I could have done a better show for those creeps! My brain actually goes over it again and again, like a skip in a record, except that I'm making it better, more relaxed . . . I say smarter things. *I actually find myself thinking of going and looking for them!*

I must be going crazy . . . these thoughts are all wrong! I am all wrong!

Speak to you later, Laura

Dear Diary, March 4, 1988

I spent yesterday with Donna, and I realized that we have nothing to say to each other any more. Sure, we chat, and she talks, but the whole time I was there, all I could think of was getting out of her house. I could feel the pure, perfect little walls closing in on me.

She actually took me to her room and closed the door, to whisper that she and Mike are going all the way soon. They're planning the whole event. Thursday night . . .? I don't remember.

So she tells me this and I'm supposed to say, 'Wow, Donna, are you sure you want to do that?'

So, I guess Donna is getting it pretty good from Bobby's best buddy, Mike. Remember him? The chewing-gum commercial? All I can say is that I hope he's good to Donna. I've always thought he was an asshole . . . but I don't have to fuck him, right?

Have fun, Donna.
Laura

I was just sitting here in my room, thinking about
Bobby. Maybe I shouldn't have told him what
happened with the truckers, because he hasn't talked
to me since then. I told him the truth, just the way he
and I talked about on New Year's Eve. We want to be
honest . . . We said we were in love . . . I only did what
I did to get out alive.

Benjamin Horne just called. Mom yelled up the
stairway that it was for me, and that it was Benjamin
Horne. My first question, before even a 'hello', was 'Is
Johnny okay? What is it?'

He said that I should sit down for a minute. I knew
Dad was home, Mom was home . . . Johnny's all right
. . . 'What is it?'

He said that Troy had been found this morning on
the tracks up by the border. His leg was broken, and
three of his shoes had come off . . . not to mention the
fact that he was completely malnourished. He hadn't
been able to find food. Benjamin said he was sure it
was Troy because of the Broken Circle brand on him.

Benjamin said that he watched the border police
shoot him. Twice to the head. He said it appeared that
someone had let him out. He promised me over the
phone that he would find this awful person and make
certain they knew what they had done to a beautiful
young horse.

I hung up.

I looked around, and everything went gray, black,
gray, black . . . I am so bad. Everywhere I turn something tells me I am an evil, wrong, bad person . . .
How could I have done such a thing to Troy?

If I weren't so fucked up and horrible, I could have

gone out, right this minute, and ridden him. Taken the both of us off into the fields where we could have survived together, somehow.

I cannot believe what is happening to me and my life! How can one day be so unbelievably precious, and another a nightmare . . . a dark dream that makes me dream of dying . . . right this very minute.

L

Not only do I love my job at the perfume counter, but I adore working with someone as cool as Ronnette. She always understands when I'm depressed and doesn't get down on me for it.

Bobby is speaking to me again and we date fairly regular – maybe twice a week at the most, or an average of, let's say, five times a month. But we used to see each other every day. Now in school we hardly hang out together. The funny thing is we were voted 'best couple' this semester by the student body.

I think we care for each other very much, but we have become objects of convenience and comfort to one another – without the love and attentiveness there used to be. We get high together a lot – mostly over at Leo's, or out by the Pearl Lakes.

The times that we get high at Leo's, especially lately, Bobby pays more attention to Shelley than he does to Leo or me.

I figure they'll have an affair ... if they aren't already secretly involved. I told Leo this the other night, which was a definite mistake on my part. I wish I could always blame the stupid things that come out of my mouth on the coke that goes up my nose, but no such luck. I had to beg him to calm down. I've never seen such violence come up so suddenly.

I don't doubt for a moment that Leo has a bad temper, but it was how much rage he felt in so little time that concerned me. Personally, I hope Bobby and Shelley are having a relationship ... I don't like the idea of being alone, at all, but worse things could happen, and I think Bobby and Shelley are good for each other. Dare I say that Leo Johnson and Laura

Palmer are cut from the same cloth . . .? Whatever, either way, my point is that Leo and I sleep together more often than Bobby and I do, and I know it is the same for Leo and Shelley.

Why do we pick up the people we do? Avoiding loneliness at almost any cost . . . picking a mate by his work schedule, his paycheck, or his abilities in the bedroom are good reasons, if you are fortunate enough to find a guy like that who is a nice guy as well.

Bobby seemed right for me. He was there. He was cute, popular, good family background . . . and he swore his love to me again and again until he finally realized that I cannot love anything right now. Falling in love is like holding a white flag out to your enemies and saying, 'We give up, we're in love, love is surrender.'

I can't do that until I know for certain that BOB is really dead. Until there is a corpse that I can kick as many times as I please. God, I hope that day comes soon.

Laura

Dear Diary,   April 10, 1988

I went to Horne's Department Store today for my introductory meeting, even though I've been there over a month. I guess I expected to learn more than I already know.

Mr Battis, the store's manager, reminds me of a large fruit – something slowly rotting . . . What is he doing here and when will he leave? Poor guy.

Mr Battis feels so guilty about screwing the boss's 'friends' that he never leaves the area around the perfume counter. I feel like he's spying on me – a constant pest who won't allow me a bullet blast or a pat on Ronnette's ass.

I remember feeling intimidated by Benjamin's office that day – the size of the room, the number of phone lines blinking constantly, his view, the size of his couch, and . . . aha . . .

Benjamin said to me that day, 'Someone from personnel will be calling you at home, Laura, to set up an introductory meeting some time soon.'

No such luck: Mr Battis is somewhat rotund and older, less distinguished than I had imagined and far less interesting to be around. Either way, I have to tell him some time quite soon that he's more annoying to everyone down here than he is helpful, and that I personally am tired of pretending to smile at his ridiculous face and boring sense of humor.

I'm sure I sound like a bitch, but hey, I've earned it. I work hard and sometimes things get to be too much for me.

I'm taking my break: be back in fifteen minutes. I need a cigarettte and a line.

I'm back. Just as I was exiting the ladies' bathroom, I saw Donna approaching my counter. *Damn*, just as I was feeling better, too.

She came up and started jabbering away about her trip out of town next week to check out colleges, and how she was going to miss Mike so much, and, 'How much does this little bottle here cost?'

I was happy to see her, but *not* happy at the same time. It upset me that she was so happy with Mike, not that I wanted him to mistreat her, but deep down I wanted to know that she liked me more, or needed my company more than his. I realize when I see it written here how selfish I am, especially when I've stopped calling her. We're not really even friends any more.

We're like everyone else, I guess. We promise that something is for ever, when it is really only as long as it takes for us to tire of it.

When she walked away, and out the door, it was like she was leaving for ever.

Laura

Dear Diary,   April 21, 1988

Ronnette just called from work to say that, even
though it's my day off, assistance isn't coming until
evening, and she needs a lot of help at the counter . . .
would I mind coming in?

In other words, tell everyone at home that you're
working late: there's a private party with Leo and
Jacques at the cabin in the woods.

Ronnette and I made up codes for things and specific
places. 'I need your assistance, right away!' means 'I
need a hit of coke, have any?' or 'Assistance is needed
at the *counter*, now!' means 'Coke is not at the cabin,
bring what you've got.'

So, Ronnette and I drove up there, and on the way I
tried to convince her that she would never be re-
cognized, never touched, and incredibly rich if she did
'it' with me. By 'it' I meant send photos of herself to
Fleshworld. I told her to make a little ad, saying you'll
send naughty tapes, panties, and pictures for a simple
fee . . . etc., etc. Get a safety-deposit box, and make up
a name with a false history - we could even have
Jacques take the photos tonight.

We had been drinking at the cabin for a couple of
hours when I told Jacques that I wanted some Polar-
oids taken of me.

The red window curtains were a large enough back-
drop, and the color was just sleazy enough so that if I
posed the right way, I'd sell a million copies.

Jacques and Leo were both excited by what I was
doing. I've found a new way to seduce them.

Ronnette saw me in action and decided perhaps it
was a good idea after all.

                                        Soon, Laura

Happy sweet sixteen to me . . .

Everything feels like a dream, a bad, very sad dream, about a little girl who all her life had a dream of her life at sweet sixteen.

God, Diary, I had such beautiful images of the boy who would love me, and never leave my side. Of how my girlfriends and I would drive my new car to the beach, strip down to our bikinis, and jump into the water. I would have the perfect body, the perfect skin, the perfect family and home – a straight-A student who is helpful and earns her own money.

I wanted my own pony, a cat, and maybe a dog. Donna Hayward would be right by my side, wearing a lacy white dress, and our boyfriends would pick us up at the front door. Our parents loved them because we had the perfect parents.

All of the above were the making of my dreams until my nightmare arrived. Not, certainly, that I thought I would have all of these 'picture perfect' moments in my life, but I still had dreams, hope that anything was possible.

I cannot tell you how special and valuable a day-dream is . . . I didn't miss it until it was *gone*. Without it I became cold, paranoid, unfriendly, and open to all sorts of horrible things.

Most of the truth you already know. Sweet sixteen is not what I thought it would be.

Bobby Briggs and I decided we would take a bit of a breather from one another – I think he is having a little affair with Shelley – no matter. I can't love Bobby the way he deserves to be loved, and it kills me inside to admit that.

I am not side by side with Donna Hayward. Something has happened to us, we grew up, *together*, but then I suddenly grew apart from her . . . Certain events aged me, made me bitter.

I see that I wrongly believed her a fool because she had not been made bitter – no one came late at night from the woods to reassure her there is no hope. No. That was my life.

I do not have a brand-new car. My parents lend me theirs. Why should I have one, in the town of Twin Peaks? There isn't really much need.

I try to work hard, but I must do more. I must work harder to redeem all my evil doings . . . my cocaine binges, all day, all night, for months. I'm an addict, and I forced Bobby to sell drugs by threatening to leave him if he didn't. I know that he would never take me back. I don't deserve him anyway. The tough, handsome exterior with a heart of gold . . . my fantasy man. I have to quit the coke.

And the sex! More than a girl my age should know. Much more. Sex that grows darker and darker – becomes an act of vengeance, rather than love.

I love to sleep with women sometimes because I know exactly how to please them and it gives me *so much control*!

I long for such strength all of the time, which again explains the cocaine. I often fear that all of my actions will send me to hell.

I had a pony. A beautiful one. Troy. His mane, a rich cinnamon color. Once again I blame myself . . . although there may be circumstances in my life that led me to believe what I did was right. It doesn't count. I led him out, caught up in my own dream of freedom. I whipped his ass, *hard*. I watched him take off . . . and I believe he looked back once, but I turned away. Somehow I already sensed what would happen to him because of me.

He was found, unfed, unshod, with a broken leg on the tracks by the border. Benjamin Horne watched him silently accept two bullets into his skull.

I have become a thief like the visitor BOB is. Stealing pride and hope, confidence . . .

My cat . . . I won't go into. It is sad enough just to think about.

I have to go.

More later, Laura

Enough of the past, and how I go on and on about the faults of the present.

I have some news that comes to me like a slap across the face. *I am pregnant.* Seven and a half weeks pregnant. No one knows but you, and the women at the clinic (I borrowed the car today to go see a doctor and be sure). I'm sure. I have so many voices in my head right now . . .

I haven't done a line of coke since last night – it seems like for ever. I wish all of my life were a dream. One grand, strange dream with many realistic plot lines and relationships, but uh, uh. This can't be the life of Laura Palmer . . . I try so hard to do well! Why?

I have no idea whose baby this is. I cannot cry any longer today because it is my sixteenth birthday, and everyone will want to know why it is that I am so upset. I am not going to tell anyone.

Laura

Dear Diary,   August 2, 1988

It has been an entire week since BOB has come
to see me. I am so numb that it actually occurred to
me the other day that I wished he would come and cut
me the way he used to. Take some of this constant
thinking again and again away, by simply bleeding it
out of me. Of course, he would not dare show up if I
wanted him to.

PAGE RIPPED OUT
(*as found*)

PAGE RIPPED OUT
(*as found*)

I think of Death these days as a companion I long to meet.

Goodbye, Laura

PAGE RIPPED OUT
(*as found*)

LITTLE BITCH.

Are you there, Bob?

ALWAYS.

Why don't you just come take me now, take my life
. . . now?

TOO EASY.

That's bullshit! I'm going insane! I can't live any
more like this! Either get out of my fucking head right
now, get out of my life, out of my home, out of my
dreams . . . or kill me!

YOU TAKE ALL OF THE FUN OUT OF IT.

So I was right from the beginning. It has always
been your goal to kill me.

*SOMETIMES, LIFE IS ABOUT WHAT
HAPPENS BEFORE DEATH. I WANTED TO
SEE WHAT COULD BE DONE.*

I'm an experiment.

YES. YOU SAID THAT ONCE BEFORE.

I've never had a chance . . .

SURE YOU HAVE.

I don't believe you.

*NOBODY DOES. THAT IS WHY YOU ARE
... FALLING.*

Falling?

INTO DARKNESS. NICE, ISN'T IT?

No.

NO?

I told you! I hate this! I hate myself, and everything
around me!

THAT'S TOO BAD.

Are you real, Bob?

*TO YOU, I AM THE ONLY REALITY THERE
IS.*

But ...

*YOU KEEP COMING BACK. YOU ALWAYS
SAY YOU'RE GOING TO STOP DOING BAD
THINGS ... YOU NEVER STOP.*

When you first came to me, I was not doing bad
things! I was a baby girl! I was nothing ... I was all
goodness ... I was happy!

INCORRECT.

I could talk to you for ever and never learn a thing.

*SOMEONE OF WISDOM IS ALWAYS MORE
DIFFICULT TO COMMUNICATE WITH. THIS
IS THE FIRE YOU MUST WALK THROUGH.*

I don't want to hear about fire.

THEN YOU DON'T WANT THE ANSWER.

Who are you . . . really?

I AM WHAT YOU FEAR I COULD BE.

Enough. I understand. It's enough. I have to go. Go
away now. Please. Just . . . leave.

HAPPY LAST DAYS, LAURA'S BABY.

I have gone insane. I won't be talking with you for a
while.

L

Dear Diary,   **August 10, 1988**

It is difficult to describe without sounding self-pity-
ing, although this is only half the truth. It was over in
only a few moments, and yet I heard all sorts of
sounds, worlds going by . . . life spinning on its heels
and running away.

The doctor came in, his large hands already wrapped
in rubber gloves, and his eyes as sterile as the room
and utensils used there.

He shook my hand. The rubber glove reminded me
of something. Was it BOB?

The last few moments with the baby were the hard-
est I've ever been through. What kind of decision
was I making? Whose baby was it?

The doctor swung his arms up into the air and said,
'Damn sleeves.' He pushed his sleeves up and went to
work.

Machines began to whir. The nurse in the room
took hold of my hand. She smiled, and the doctor
leaned between my spread legs and hovered there for a
moment; he looked down at me and said, 'There will
be some discomfort.'

And so I closed my eyes and took hold of the
nurse's hand. I wished that whoever this child was
would come back when the time is right.

*When there is a marriage. A union that you were born
of, not responsible for. You, child, should be a gift to
those who are ready, not a burden like so many others
before you. Come back, child, when I am no longer a
child myself.*

                                        Laura

Dear Diary,   August 10, 1988

I cried all the way back from the clinic and thought
of all the things that had happened to me, or that I had
let happen to me, within the past few months. I wish
Maddy could have been here with me. I almost called
to ask her if she would come, but decided not to.

My only real sense of gratification came from the
fact that as of today, one a.m., I am nineteen days
sober. No coke. It has been much harder than I ever
thought it would be. Sometimes simply out of habit
I'll check the bedpost for any remaining film on the
paraphernalia I still keep in the space there.

By the way, I forgot to tell you Norma called me a
couple of days ago, and we're meeting tomorrow to
discuss my idea for helping the elderly of Twin Peaks.
I hope it all works out because this could be beneficial
to the town as well as my sobriety.

Once I got home I realized how much pain I was in.
I didn't think I would even make it up the stairs to my
room. Mom caught up to me instantly and said, 'So,
how'd it go?'

'The interview was just fine, Mom.'

I gripped the banister tightly and told her I was
heading to bed early. I could feel her watching me as I
went up, step by step. Just as I was at the top of the
staircase Mom called up to me and said that I had had
a phone call from cousin Maddy. I stood there in awe.
Maddy had heard me calling to her.

In that same moment I was aware of Mom's stare –
pure jealousy at my back.

I've got to rest.

                                                   Laura

Dear Diary,   August 16, 1988
                                         3:15 a.m.

It has been some time now since the two of us have
met this late at night.

Sobriety is a bitch. I've never been more paranoid
than I have been these past few days. I feel like I've
lost all of my friends because I'm sober.

Ronnette and I don't talk the way we used to,
especially at work, and I am not notified of parties
taking place up at the cabin any more.

Bobby never really calls. *I call him!* How weird is
that! He seems to be fine without me, which makes me
feel like everyone will notice that and stop dealing
with me altogether. I wonder, am I the bad influence
BOB always tells me I am?

Does my sobriety mean I will end up totally alone?
Even my new friend Harold Smith

PAGE RIPPED OUT
(*as found*)

Dear Diary,   August 20, 1988
                               5:20 a.m.

It is very dark in my room right now, and I am only writing to you by the glow of the night-light.

I do not want anyone to see me awake. I feel so scared.

I just had a nightmare and now I'm sweating like crazy and can hardly breathe. In the dream everyone in the world was taking drugs, but I had stopped. I don't know why . . . maybe it made me feel better. I think I thought it was the right thing to do.

As soon as I'd stopped, I became invisible. I broke up into empty space and floated around Twin Peaks . . . through school . . . No one noticed me, *no one*! I ran into a classroom and saw Donna. I walked right up to her and screamed in her face, but she didn't hear me. Bobby and Shelley were walking toward me in the hall. They were speaking to each other and they walked *right through me*! When I turned to go after them, I saw Leo and Jacques by the drinking fountain. *Even they didn't see me!*

I couldn't get anyone's attention or make them believe that I mattered because to them I didn't. They couldn't see me because *I* was sober.

The whole dream seemed so real. I felt so alone.

When I looked up to check the light from the hallway, there outside the window, looking in at me, laughing (his sounds and laughter muted by the glass), was BOB! Son of a bitch!

I saw his face across the room, highlighted by the orangeish glow of my night-light. Only a pane of glass separated us. He kept laughing and then lowered him-

209

self, slowly, out of the square that is my window. I
was unable to rest until the sun rose and the window
held the light that does not allow him to return.

Love, Laura

Mr Battis had asked that I meet with him in his
office at five-thirty. At five-fifteen I told Ronnette
that I should go, but I'd be back as soon as I could to
help her unload the new products.

I was left alone in Battis's office for several minutes.
I took a seat in the chair in front of his desk.

When Mr Battis walked in, he took a quick look at
me and smiled. He liked me, I knew that, but now it
was even more obvious.

Mr Battis took two steps toward his window and
looked out between the curtains.

'Something tells me that you are in the market for a
better job?'

'Yes.' I crossed my legs. 'That's true.'

Still looking out the window, he said, 'I believe we
have the job for you.'

'And what would that be, Mr Battis?' I said.

'A hostess . . . with room to grow.'

'A hostess?'

'Can you dance, Miss Palmer?'

'Amory, I can do a lot of things.'

'Then you can make a lot of money.'

Mr Battis told me to meet him here next Saturday
and we (Ronnette included) would go to a place across
the border called One-Eyed Jack's.

I thanked him and left his office. Walking back to
the perfume counter, I made the decision that sobriety
was not for me.

Ronnette said she'd cover for me awhile. I took her
bullet back to the storage room. I took my hits, turned

to leave, and there was BOB, crouched in the corner, smiling victoriously.

New game, Laura

Dear Diary,   August 23, 1988

I feel so much better with cocaine back in my life!

I've been meaning to tell you what became of my meeting with Norma. I had been thinking about the very best way to help the elderly who find it difficult to leave the house.

I would deliver meals to the elderly people in the area who couldn't get out for a hot meal. I told her the name of the program could be Meals on Wheels.

Norma loved the idea and said she would make a few calls to people at city hall and maybe the hospital. We could find the best recipients that way, without doing much footwork. Norma agreed to provide the meals, two a day, four times a week. All profits to go fifty-fifty. I deliver them to the door, and maybe I'll regain some confidence . . . Or am I confident? Or am I so fucked up on coke that I can't tell?

So, today, I came to pick up two meals at the diner.

I was helping Norma pull the meals from the oven when Josie Packard came in.

She and Norma had a quick talk, during which Josie became a bit upset, emotional. Norma called me over and explained that Josie was being hassled at the mill again about her English . . . I could tell she was embarrassed by it.

I told her that I'd love to give her English lessons if she'd like.

Norma gave me a smile and a pat on the shoulder. Josie stepped forward and said, 'I'd be more than happy to pay you for these services.'

I shook her hand and she said that her first available day was next Monday evening. I told her that was fine. I would see her Monday.

I left the diner with the meals. I had to deliver them and get up to Johnny Horne's in forty-five minutes.

I went to Mrs Tremond's apartment first. I left the tray at the front door along with the appropriate note, and a request for a house key of my own.

Harold Smith was my other delivery. As I think I told you, he's an interesting man. Very handsome. Apparently he was a botanist. For some reason he can't remember, he awoke one morning to find himself an agoraphobic. He believes death is just outside the door, and that late at night it calls to him from outside like a strange bird.

He invited me in but I was already late so I told him I'd have to take a rain check.

I got up to the Hornes' and they were all ready to leave. I told them to have a good time, that Johnny and I would be fine, not to worry.

I convinced Bobby to drop some coke off for me, and Johnny and I spent the evening reading his story-books and eating ice cream.

More later, Laura

PAGE RIPPED OUT
(*as found*)

PAGE RIPPED OUT
(*as found*)

Dear Diary,   August 31, 1988

I just reread yesterday's entry and I suddenly feel
very embarrassed about being alive. The girl who
received this diary on her twelfth birthday has been
dead for years, and I who took her place have done
nothing but make a mockery of the dreams she once had.
I'm sixteen years old, I'm a cocaine addict, a prostitute
who fucks her father's employers, not to mention half
the fucking town, and the only difference from last week
is that now I'm getting paid for it. My life is whatever
the other person in the room wants it to be.

Therefore, when I am alone, my life is nothing.

I dreamed last night that I was outside Jacques's cabin
in the woods, and I was trying to find a way inside.
There was no front door, only a window, *identical to
the one in my bedroom*. I looked through the window
and saw Waldo flying back and forth very, very slowly.
It was as if he were moving in slow motion, but I
could tell that he was panicked. He called out, 'Laura,
Laura,' as if in warning ... And suddenly BOB
stepped into the square of the window and grabbed
Waldo in his hands. BOB turned to me smiling, and
with one squeeze, crushed Waldo to death.

I backed away from the window and ran from the
house as fast as I could. No matter where I turned the
house was always in front of me and each time I saw
BOB he was closer to climbing out of the window.

I fell to my knees. Everything went silent. I looked
up and there, thirty feet in front of me, *was a gigantic
owl*. As I look back now, I am still unsure. 'Was he a
friend or an enemy?'

We stood staring at each other for a long time. It felt
as if he wanted to say something, but he did not.

I awoke hoping that what the Log Lady said, 'Owls are sometimes big,' referred to tonight and meant that something good was going to happen to me. Now that I'm working at One-Eyed Jack's I could use a good omen. I will pay attention to everything the way the Log Lady told me I should. I suspect that this will be the first of many things I will need to pay close attention to.

Laura

P.S. I think that in order to ensure my privacy I will need to start a second diary, one that if found will give the intruder 'the Laura' that everyone thinks lives inside of me.

I will have to spend time filling its pages. I wonder if life is still something I can make up.

Dear Diary,   November 13, 1988

I was up at the Hornes' having a session with Johnny. One of his doctors, Dr Lawrence Jacoby, joined us to shoot a few rubber buffalo.

I was immediately aware of Lawrence's attraction to me, not that that was the issue, but where his attraction came from *was*.

He had fallen in love with the '*two Lauras*', the very reasons for which I wanted so desperately to die. What I considered a curse, he found enticing and honest. He did not mock my pain. *He accepted it*.

So Dr Jacoby and I began to meet secretly at his office. He just lets me talk and I will sometimes try to shock him with the details of my darker self, yet he continues to accept them, accept me, always recognizing that the lighter part of me never wanted to do them in the first place. And so he forgives me. I know this may sound very sick and mean, perhaps, but I am almost consumed, at times, with hatred for him because never has he turned to me and confirmed my deepest fears – that I am becoming like BOB – bad.

Maybe it is the way he says it is: I have simply forgotten how to be loved.

                                        Laura

Dear Diary,   January 13, 1989

I haven't been writing to you because Dr Jacoby
gave me a pretty hot-pink tape recorder for Christmas.
He said that it might help me to talk into it. I send
him the tapes after I have listened to them myself. I
find that even though I'm still very sad, listening to
the tapes and all that they say helps me feel that the
problems spoken on them are not my own.

I would write more often, but with all my work and
the other diary I must keep 'pleasantly updated', I
have hardly any time to be as honest as I am with you.

I will write more when I can.

                                                   Laura

Dear Diary, March 27, 1989

I had been promising to spend a few moments with Harold for weeks now, and finally today I was able to do so.

His apartment is small and filled with books from the toilet tank to the top of the fridge. I think he has to keep reading these stories because he so rarely has any stories of his own.

I like to play with Harold sometimes. I like the way he hangs on my every word as I describe some of my adventures. In particular those from One-Eyed Jack's (where, by the way, Jacques works as a blackjack dealer). My stories stimulate Harold. I know that. But yet he reacts almost violently, and with fear, when I make advances toward him, no matter how mild. I love Harold's tenderness and most often feel wonderful when I am with him and when I think about him. But sometimes I hate myself more than you can imagine for the aroused feelings I get when I see Harold's frightened face, which must be the same thing BOB sees when he looks at me. The prey, cornered . . . so degraded . . . made a toy. I am noticing that more and more, and I think BOB is, too, when he visits me, that I cannot hurt or be hurt enough lately.

Laura

Dear Diary, June 4, 1989

I have been working with Josie on her English lessons for a while now and she shows very few signs of improvement or efforts to improve. I know that Josie was a dancer and a prostitute in Hong Kong when Andrew fell in love with her and saved her life by bringing her here six years ago, and I think she still has more of that lifestyle in her than most realize. She's treating our sessions more like poorly executed seductions and the more she comes on to me the less I respect her. It's not that she's all over me. It's different than that . . . She mentions Bobby a lot and I can tell she is jealous of him. She makes too many insinuations about my sexual goings-on for me to believe she is not a darker person than the town thinks. Poor Sheriff Truman.

Laura

P.S. It makes me sick how every time I do something good I always end up – pardon the pun – getting fucked.

Dear Diary, August 6, 1989

Norma had taken care of almost all the deliveries that week, but asked if I would handle Mr Penderghast since she had to go visit her husband, Hank, in prison that afternoon. I told her I'd be happy to.

I have sixteen keys on my key chain other than the five that are my own. Every so often, I daydream of the fantastic access I have to homes that are not my own. I understand the thrill a burglar must feel upon entering an apartment and suddenly being able to decide that anything in sight is his own.

Mr Penderghast is the most trusting and the most kind of any of the elderly I deliver to. I inserted the key into his door and entered quietly. I could hear the television on in his bedroom and called out to him that I was there.

He did not answer.

When I found him, he was behind his bedroom door, his hands still tight to the doorknob as if he had used it as a support in his attempt to move, simply, through his own house. For a man who was so gentle, I thought it was a shame that he should die wearing such an expression of struggle. The look in his eyes and the shape of his mouth told me he felt left behind and betrayed by his friends. I waited almost an hour before I phoned for the ambulance. I sat down next to him and watched him, so still, holding death.

I do not think that hour there told me anything I could not have imagined myself, but being there, in that silence, gave me hope that at least there are no wars after death.

I have seen more death than I have seen life. Some-

times even the most tired clichés apply. I believe I
am merely living my life in order to die.

Laura

Dear Diary,

In the middle of my shift last night at One-Eyed Jack's, I left my room and went into the office. I wanted to use the bathroom there because it had a lock on it. I had come down so hard that I needed more than just a bullet hit, I needed a couple of big fat lines . . . When I exited the bathroom I used the other door which connects to Blackie's room. She was on the bed with a tourniquet on her arm shooting heroin. I may be fucked up, but I don't shoot that shit up my arm. That's an idiot's drug.

Blackie leaned her head back, having obviously just caught the high. I said to her directly, 'I came in here for my money.'

Euphoric, and a bit patronizingly, she said, 'You'll get it tonight.'

'That's what you told me last night.' I paused. 'Maybe if you stopped shooting that shit up your arm you wouldn't forget the things you've said.'

Blackie stood up, settling into her high, and said that she was sick of my little-girl attitude and that I should grow up. She also added that she thought I should stop 'frolicking in the snow' . . . that the customers were beginning to notice. I told her that was ridiculous, the customers hadn't noticed anything but better sex and better service than they'd ever had there before.

'But they haven't fucked me yet,' Blackie replied.

I hesitated purposely, then said, 'Oh, I thought that fucking you was punishment for those who . . .'

Blackie interrupted me with a slap across the face. She looked me in the eye and said, 'I'm going to teach you a thing or two about fucking right now.'

I smiled the way BOB would and thought to myself, *I'll be the one teaching the lesson.*

By the time I left Blackie, she was on the floor, naked except for her jewelry, and was humiliated because I had been able to take total control and show her things she had never thought possible. I took her into a very dark erotic place . . . but I left her there alone.

As I opened the door Blackie threw her final, and only remaining, punch.

'You better watch that cocaine use, Laura. It could get you fired.'

I knew right then that it was to be my last night at One-Eyed Jack's.

Laura

P.S. I'm going to have to tell the world about Benjamin.

Dear Diary,   October 10, 1989

I phoned Josie and told her I wouldn't be able to make the lesson that night until at least ten o'clock. She said that was fine and that she would be waiting for me.

That night I took advantage of the fact that someone wanted me so badly. And yet I found myself, as always, instructing my partner on how to please me. This experience, in particular, left me feeling empty and angry, and without respect for yet another person in town.

Laura

P.S. On the way home from Josie's I had a horrible vision of little Danielle running up to me to explain that BOB had been visiting her. He had told her I had sent him to her. When I came out of the vision, I realized that BOB had not come to visit me in over a week . . . I hoped that this was only a vision, and not a premonition. Perhaps I should warn Danielle . . .

Dear Diary,

It's Hallowe'en. No mask necessary.

Blackie's sister, Nancy, from One-Eyed Jack's, brought my clothes and the money they owed me stuffed into a plastic pumpkin. She asked if she could talk to me outside for a moment because

PAGE RIPPED OUT
(as found)

I spent the afternoon with Dr Jacoby at his office. He wanted to see me and go over what I had said to him on my tapes. He wanted to hear more about James Hurley and the fact that I had mentioned going sober because of him. I told him James was someone I had known for a long time, although not so well. I told him I had fallen in love with his purity and the idea that if I was strong enough I could let James take me out of this darkness. I told him that it was a secret relationship only because I had wanted it that way. Donna knows. But the three of us are friends at school so I know she won't tell Bobby.

I told Dr Jacoby how hard it had been for me lately with everything getting so close, and how I finally felt certain that James was my last chance for light.

I feel like a fake, I told him, even though I was Homecoming Queen. I had such a story behind my smile in the photos and at the football game as well. I still felt the hands and the mouths of the men I had been with hours before the photo was taken. I told him I had worn the same panties just in case BOB came. I told him it felt like the school and the town and the world were mocking me by voting me Homecoming Queen . . . How could they not see how I was being swallowed up by pain? How dare they make me a spectacle like that and ask me to smile again and again and again!

At the game Bobby was the hero he wanted to be, but from the stands I could hardly make him out on the field. Everything seemed far away and muted, as if the blood rushing through my head hushed all the sounds except for my heartbeat and my breathing, which seemed labored, erratic.

I told him I had been having awful nightmares. All of them about the woods, the paths, the tree, foot-prints, the sounds of an owl ... I felt death in these dreams and I also felt lust. Lust like I had known when it was fresh to me and it wasn't tired and worn-out and bettered only by violence.

I did have one dream, *the worst*, about water. In the dream I was standing at the water's edge and the sky was very, very dark, but reflected on the surface of the water was the sky filled with white clouds and a deep blue color. I remember thinking in the dream that if I dove in and swam far enough, I might come up in another world that was not filled with so much badness ... so much hatred. When I did dive in, I remember swimming half the length of the lake – I think it was a lake – only to be pulled down by a hand as it grabbed my wrist and took me deeper and deeper and deeper. I told him I thought that hand was BOB's.

I told Dr Jacoby that the last time I had seen Leo and Jacques had not been very nice. We had all been fooling around, and they had tied me up in this chair, but I started to get this feeling of claustrophobia ... restriction. I started to panic and hyperventilate and I tried to explain what was happening but it was difficult to speak and no one realized I was being serious. I started to get very lightheaded and there were flashes of light in my eyes and I was finally able to scream out for them to stop. This was not all right ... I was not all right. We had been playing one of the games we play a lot where I am trapped in a cabin far, far away from any help and that I am a virgin and they are men who have been sent from a strange and erotic place to take my virginity and to punish me for resisting them. And so Leo heard me say this was not all right, but he thought it was part of the game and he said, 'Oh, is the little virgin scared?' It went on like that and I started rocking the chair back and forth and I guess Leo was really into it, as was Jacques, and Leo got a little crazy and he hit me, hard ... too hard. My ears rang. I began to cry. It wasn't until then that Jacques said, 'Wait a minute, she's not okay.' They untied me and I ran home without saying a word.

Leo's slap had left an ugly bruise on my cheek. I had to tell my parents that this horrible black and blue mark came from when I was carrying a dinner from Harold's apartment.

I told Dr Jacoby I missed Donna and I wished that she and Ronnette would like each other. I wish that we could all be friends so I wouldn't have to hide anything from anyone.

I told him about how I had gone to Harold's last week, *really fucked up*, and how scared I made him by coming on to him pretty heavy. And then, basically because he could not leave his house, *forced* him to have sex with me.

I told Dr Jacoby that I cried for hours afterward because I felt so horrible. It took Harold almost an hour to talk to me because I had made him scared, even in his own home, his only refuge. And then I told Dr Jacoby that half the time I hated it and the rest of the time it made me feel strong and hot between the legs.

On the way out of Harold's, Mrs Tremond's grandson, Pierre, saw me and came up to me and pulled a gold coin out of my ear and walked away.

I told him that BOB was getting very, very close and that I was trying as hard as I could to write about him to find out what he was, who he was, before he

235

could get to me. I had been writing so much about him in my diary in poems and dreams, and each time I did it I would see him at my window or feel him coming closer, but I wasn't sure if it was paranoia . . . I just wanted to be normal. I just want to be like everybody else. I don't like having to be careful of who to talk to because someone might hate me if they knew the truth about me, about how dirty I am. And how somehow, I don't remember it, but, somehow everyday I asked to be treated this way. It always happens, so it must be something I don't realize I say, or something I think. I told him how I went to my safety-deposit box and how I saw the drug money there and I had a fantasy about taking it and running away for ever. But I didn't deserve that. I deserved to stay here. I had done something wrong. My heart hurt so badly, but I knew I had to stay.

I took the responses from my ad in *Fleshworld* home with me and stayed up all night putting pictures of me and my panties into envelopes . . . and how I had to keep getting higher and higher on coke so I wouldn't break down and cry and I didn't want anyone to hear my cries because they didn't matter to them anyway. *They never have.*

Love, Laura

PAGE RIPPED OUT
(*as found*)

PAGE RIPPED OUT
(*as found*)

Dear Diary, [undated]

I know who he is. I know exactly who and what BOB is, and I have to tell everyone. I have to tell someone and make them believe.

Someone has torn pages out of my diary, pages that help me realize maybe ... pages with my poems, pages of writing, *private pages*.

I'm so afraid of death.

I'm so afraid that no one will believe me until after I have taken the seat that I fear has been saved for me in the darkness. Please don't hate me. I never meant to see the small hills and the fire. I never meant to see him or let him in.

Please, Diary, help me explain to everyone that I did not want what I have become. I did not want to have certain memories and realizations of him. I only did what any of us can do, in any situation ...

My very best.

Love, Laura

P.S. I'm giving you to Harold for safekeeping. I hope I see you again. I can't stay sober any more. I just can't. I have to be numb.

**THE PRECEDING WAS
LAURA'S LAST ENTRY.
SHE WAS FOUND DEAD
JUST DAYS LATER.**

FOR THE BEST IN PAPERBACKS, LOOK FOR THE

In every corner of the world, on every subject under the sun, Penguin represents quality and variety – the very best in publishing today.

For complete information about books available from Penguin – including Puffins, Penguin Classics and Arkana – and how to order them, write to us at the appropriate address below. Please note that for copyright reasons the selection of books varies from country to country.

In the United Kingdom: Please write to *Dept E.P., Penguin Books Ltd, Harmondsworth, Middlesex, UB7 0DA.*

If you have any difficulty in obtaining a title, please send your order with the correct money, plus ten per cent for postage and packaging, to *PO Box No 11, West Drayton, Middlesex*

In the United States: Please write to *Dept BA, Penguin, 299 Murray Hill Parkway, East Rutherford, New Jersey 07073*

In Canada: Please write to *Penguin Books Canada Ltd, 2801 John Street, Markham, Ontario L3R 1B4*

In Australia: Please write to the *Marketing Department, Penguin Books Australia Ltd, P.O. Box 257, Ringwood, Victoria 3134*

In New Zealand: Please write to the *Marketing Department, Penguin Books (NZ) Ltd, Private Bag, Takapuna, Auckland 9*

In India: Please write to *Penguin Overseas Ltd, 706 Eros Apartments, 56 Nehru Place, New Delhi, 110019*

In the Netherlands: Please write to *Penguin Books Netherlands B.V., Postbus 195, NL–1380AD Weesp*

In West Germany: Please write to *Penguin Books Ltd, Friedrichstrasse 10–12, D–6000 Frankfurt/Main 1*

In Spain: Please write to *Longman Penguin España, Calle San Nicolas 15, E–28013 Madrid*

In Italy: Please write to *Penguin Italia s.r.l., Via Como 4, I-20096 Pioltello (Milano)*

In France: Please write to *Penguin Books Ltd, 39 Rue de Montmorency, F-75003 Paris*

In Japan: Please write to *Longman Penguin Japan Co Ltd, Yamaguchi Building, 2–12 -9 Kanda Jimbocho, Chiyoda-Ku, Tokyo 101*

FOR THE BEST IN PAPERBACKS, LOOK FOR THE 🐧

PENGUIN BESTSELLERS

Gorillas in the Mist Dian Fossey

For thirteen years Dian Fossey lived among the gorillas of the Virunga Mountains in Africa, defending them from brutal slaughter by poachers. In 1985 she was herself brutally murdered. *Gorillas in the Mist* is her story. 'Fascinating' – Paul Theroux

Presumed Innocent Scott Turow

The No. 1 International Bestseller. 'One of the most enthralling novels I have read in a long, long time' – Pat Conroy. 'If you start *Presumed Innocent* you will finish it … it grips like an octopus' – *Sunday Times*

The Second Rumpole Omnibus John Mortimer

Horace Rumpole turns down yet another invitation to exchange the joys and sorrows of life as an Old Bailey hack for the delights of the sunshine state and returns again in *Rumpole for the Defence*, *Rumpole and the Golden Thread* and *Rumpole's Last Case*.

Pearls Celia Brayfield

The Bourton sisters were beautiful. They were rich. They were famous. They were powerful. Then one morning they wake up to find a priceless pearl hidden under their pillows. Why? 'Readers will devour it' – *Independent*

Spring of the Ram Dorothy Dunnett
Volume 2 in the *House of Niccolò* series

Niccolò has now travelled as far as the frontier of Islam in order to establish the Silk Route for the Charetty empire. Beset by illness, feuds and the machinations of his rivals, he must use his most Machiavellian schemes to survive…

The New Confessions William Boyd

The outrageous, hilarious autobiography of John James Todd, a Scotsman born in 1899 and one of the great self-appointed (and failed) geniuses of the twentieth century. 'Brilliant ... a Citizen Kane of a novel' – *Daily Telegraph*

The House of Stairs Barbara Vine

'A masterly and hypnotic synthesis of past, present and terrifying future ... compelling and disturbing' – *Sunday Times*. 'Not only ... a quietly smouldering suspense novel but also ... an accurately atmospheric portrayal of London in the heady '60s. Literally unputdownable' – *Time Out*

Summer's Lease John Mortimer

'It's high summer, high comedy too, when Molly drags her amiably bickering family to a rented Tuscan villa for the hols ... With a cosy fluency of wit, Mortimer charms us into his urbane tangle of clues...' – *Mail on Sunday*. 'Superb' – Ruth Rendell

Touch Elmore Leonard

'I bleed from five wounds and heal people, but I've never been in love. Isn't that something?' They call him Juvenal, and he's a wanted man in downtown Detroit... 'Discover Leonard for yourself – he's something else' – *Daily Mail*

Story of My Life Jay McInerney

'The first year I was in New York I didn't do anything but guys and blow...' 'The leader of the pack' – *Time Out*. 'Fast and sharp ... a very good novel indeed' – *Observer*

Riding the Iron Rooster Paul Theroux

An eye-opening and entertaining account of travels in old and new China, from the author of *The Great Railway Bazaar*. 'Mr Theroux cannot write badly ... in the course of a year there was almost no train in the vast Chinese rail network on which he did not travel' – Ludovic Kennedy

Touched by Angels Derek Jameson

His greatest story yet – his own. 'My story is simple enough. I grew up poor and hungry on the streets of London's East End and decided at an early age it was better to be rich and successful.'

The Rich are Different Susan Howatch

Wealth is power – and all power corrupts. 'A superb saga, with all the bestselling ingredients – love, hate, death, murder, and a hell of a lot of passion' – *Daily Mirror*

The Cold Moons Aeron Clement

For a hundred generations the badgers of Cilgwyn had lived in harmony with nature – until a dying stranger limped into their midst, warning of the coming of men. Men whose scent had inexplicably terrified him, men armed with rifles and poison gas...

The Return of Heroic Failures Stephen Pile

The runaway success of *The Book of Heroic Failures* was a severe embarrassment to its author. From the song-free Korean version of *The Sound of Music* to the least successful attempt to tranquillize an animal, his hilarious sequel plumbs new depths of human incompetence.

A Sense of Guilt   Andrea Newman

The sensational new novel by the author of *A Bouquet of Barbed Wire*. 'How pleasant life would be, he reflected, if he could have all three of them ... the virgin, the mother and the whore.' 'From the first toe-tingling sentence ... I couldn't put this bulky, breathless beanfeast of a novel down' – *Daily Mail*

Nice Work   David Lodge

'The campus novel meets the industrial novel ... compulsive reading' – David Profumo in the *Daily Telegraph*. 'A work of immense intelligence, informative, disturbing and diverting ... one of the best novelists of his generation' – Anthony Burgess in the *Observer*

Difficulties With Girls   Kingsley Amis

Last seen in *Take a Girl Like You*, Patrick Standish and Jenny, née Bunn, are now married and up-and-coming south of the Thames. Unfortunately, like his neighbours, Patrick continues to have difficulties with girls ... 'Very funny ... vintage Amis' – *Guardian*

The Looney   Spike Milligan

Would Mick Looney's father lie on his HP deathbed? Well, he had to lie somewhere. When he told Mick that they are the descendants of the Kings of Ireland, was he telling the truth? If he was, why is Mick mixing cement in the rain in Kilburn? 'Hysterical' – *Time Out*

In the Midday Sun   Guy Bellamy

On the sun-soaked Costa del Sol three fugitive brothers from England – bank robber, tax evader and layabout – contemplate the female form and the shape of things to come. But Matthew, Mark and Daniel have spent far too long in the midday sun ... 'The blue skies blacken very funnily indeed' – *Mail on Sunday*

PENGUIN BESTSELLERS

A Fatal Inversion Barbara Vine

Ten years after the young people camped at Wyvis Hall, the bodies of a woman and child are found in the animal cemetery. But which woman? And whose child? 'Impossible to put down' – Anita Brookner. 'I defy anyone to guess the conclusion' – *Daily Telegraph*

The Favoured Child Philippa Gregory

The gripping new bestseller from the author of *Wideacre*. Wideacre Hall is a smoke-blackened ruin, but in the Dower House two children are being raised in protected innocence – equal claimants to the Wideacre inheritance. Only one can be the favoured child. Only one can be Beatrice Lacey's true heir...

Crimson Joy Robert B. Parker

Just because all the victims are black women doesn't necessarily make the killer racist or sexist. Just because he sends Quirk a letter saying he's a cop doesn't mean it's true. *Crimson Joy* pits Frank Spenser against a psychopath.

Oscar Wilde Richard Ellmann

'Exquisite critical sense, wide and deep learning, and profound humanity ... a great subject and a great book' – Anthony Burgess in the *Observer*. 'The witty subject has found a witty biographer' – Claire Tomalin in the *Independent*

O-Zone Paul Theroux

It's New Year in paranoid, computer-rich New York, and a group of Owners has jet-rotored out to party in O-Zone, the radioactive wasteland where the people do not officially exist. 'Extremely exciting ... as ferocious and as well-written as *The Mosquito Coast*, and that's saying something' – *The Times*

FOR THE BEST IN PAPERBACKS, LOOK FOR THE 🐧

CRIME AND MYSTERY IN PENGUIN

The Blunderer Patricia Highsmith

Walter Stackhouse wishes his wife was dead. His wish comes true when Clara's body is found at the bottom of a cliff. But there are uncanny similarities between her death and that of a woman called Helen Kimmel – murdered by her husband... 'Almost unputdownable' – *Observer*

Farewell, My Lovely Raymond Chandler

Moose Malloy was a big man but not more than six feet five inches tall and not wider than a beer truck. He looked about as inconspicuous as a tarantula on a slice of angel food. Marlowe's greatest case, Chandler's greatest book.

Death's Bright Angel Janet Neel

At Britex Fabrics Francesca Wilson's economic investigation and John McLeish's murder inquiry are getting inextricably confused – with an American senator, a pop star and the Bach Choir as well as each other... 'A brilliant début ... sharp, intelligent and amusing' – *Independent*

Crimson Joy Robert B. Parker

Just because all the victims are black women doesn't necessarily make the killer racist or sexist. Just because he sends Quirk a letter saying he's a cop doesn't mean it's true. *Crimson Joy* pits Frank Spenser against a psychopath.